False Idols

and Other Short Stories

TONY LAROCCA

ISBN-10: 0989416003
ISBN-13: 978-0-9894160-0-9

www.EgotisticalProductions.com

10 9 8 7 6 5 4 3 2

CONTENTS

AD AWARE

Death by midlife crisis, Richard Bringham thought as he tumbled through the void. *Please, don't let them put that on my tombstone.* He had never expected death to be so… annoying. If he had only lived, he could have sued Fun–Sport JetPaks for incorrectly labeling their product. It should have read, "Not to be purchased by men in their forties hell–bent on proving —"

"Mister Bringham," someone said in the darkness, "please open your eyes."

Richard jerked as the voice sluiced away the bliss of oblivion. He heard the whine of machinery, and felt his limbs sting with pins and needles. He was corporal again, and his burning lungs demanded that he breathe. He gasped, opening his eyes.

The reek of ammonia flooded his sinuses. He lay on his back, suspended by an antigravity harness within a vast, mint–green chamber. An array of Nightingales hovered above, scanning him with flickering rays of blue light. He raised his head an inch, and was rewarded with a stomach–churning vertigo.

A man with a smooth face and glistening spectacles loomed into Richard's view. "Welcome back from the abyss," he said, arching his eyebrows on the last word. There was a "W.E." embroidered on his white coat: the insignia of a Wellness Extraspecialist.

Richard's mind spun. There were life lessons here, he realized: Do not JetPak through Times Square, even if some schmuck from marketing dares you. Remember that skyscraper canyons create wind tunnels. When you lose control and find yourself tossed around like God's beanbag, please feel free to wet yourself. But most important of all, stay away from Port Mort Kola billboards, especially if they are giant LCD displays designed to be seen from space, because it will hurt and hurt bad when you smash into one. He tried to speak with the numb piece of meat that was his tongue. "How?" he mumbled. "Crash."

"Yes," the W.E. said. "You were electrocuted, I'm afraid. It cooked your heart beyond repair." He grinned. "But you'll be happy to know we've replaced it with a fully functional, biomechanical one that's top of the line."

It took a moment for the words to sink into Richard's addled brain. His eyes widened as understanding brought with it a pang of anxiety. "Money," he said, "can't afford..."

"Ah, ah, ah, don't worry about that," the W.E. said. "Americana Coverage: free health care for all, no matter the need, no matter the cost. We cover everyone."

The fear in Richard's mind waned. "Free," he said.

"Just about," said the doctor. He bowed from the waist. "Call me Doctor Hank. Perhaps you've seen my face on the Americana posters conveniently located..."

Richard smiled as he sank back onto his pillow, ignoring the idiot's prattle. He was alive, and he was covered. What else mattered?

"Free," he whispered.

"Port Mort Kola! Port Mort Kola! Port Mort Kola!"

Richard woke to the sound of his own screams. He slumped back onto sweat–damped sheets.

Two weeks had passed since the accident. Two weeks, and the nightmares would not stop, but all Doctor Hank offered in the way of help was psychobabble. "The billboard was the last thing you saw before death," the quack insisted. "It's only natural for the subconscious to replay its tragedy." Richard had no stomach for that kind of crap. In fact, he wanted to wring the W.E. by his patronizing neck.

He blinked. His thoughts had taken him out of his bedroom, down the hall, and into the kitchen. He sank to his knees on the cold, tiled floor, trembling. He was going insane. He was losing his mind.

He was thirsty.

Christ, he was thirsty.

He opened the Suck It 2 Me. They were still in there, of course, twelve of them. They sat innocently on the shelf. Richard caressed one, feeling the cool, sleek glass in his hand. He read the label: Port Mort Kola. He yanked it out of the refrigerator, tore off the cap, and chugged it down. The empty bottle fell from his fingers and shattered on the floor as he grabbed another, then another, and then another. He let out a long, triumphant belch, the sticky Kola dribbling down his chin.

After a few minutes, the refrigerator spoke up. "Excuse me, sir," it said, "but you're letting all the cold air out."

Richard ignored it as a chill settled over him. He could not see any more bottles. He tore the shelves out, throwing moldy leftovers and condiments to the floor.

"More Port Mort," he said. His throat burned.

"May I suggest some Fruity Fun Punch?" the Suck It 2 Me asked. "It's nutritious, tastes great, and keeps you regular, all for one credit."

"More Port Mort."

"I'm sorry, sir, but I'm out," said the refrigerator. "If you'd insert only four credits, I'll have another twelve–pack sucked to me in a jiffy." Richard slammed the door. He sniffed. There was some sweet, sweet Kola somewhere close. He fell to the floor amongst the shards of broken bottles. A drop here, a drop there. He could sense them. He stuck out his tongue and lapped up the delicious Port Mort Kola, garnished with just a touch of glass.

A month later, Richard waddled into the Wellness Clinic. His bloodshot eyes were downcast, staring with guilt at his tremendous gut. He leaned against the wall, and waited for his Wellness Extraspecialist's tirade.

"Richard," said Doctor Hank as he strolled into the room, "it seems you have put on weight." He stumbled backward as Richard leaped at him, grabbing the W.E. by his collar.

"You've got to help me, Doc," he said. "I'm going insane."

A benign, pitying smile came to Doctor Hank's face. He clapped his hands, and the lights dimmed. The examination table inflated, and molded itself into a couch. "Fortunately for you, your Americana Wellness Extraspecialist is trained for everything," he said, pulling a small pad out of his coat. "Please, tell me what the problem is."

Richard sank onto the couch. He closed his eyes, and recounted his recurring nightmare:

"I crawl through the desert," he said. "The sand burns my skin. I'm dying of thirst. On the horizon, I see an oasis. I run to it and drink, but the water is bitter, and stings my throat like rotten grapefruit juice. I look up, and a camel is doing its business in it. Nauseous, I crawl to the next oasis. It's full of milk — sweet, cool milk. But by the time I get there, it's moldy, and reeks of decrepit cheese. Green blobs float in it. I sally forth, and finally I reach another oasis. This time it's Port Mort Kola. I really don't like Port Mort, but of course I drink it, and it's the most refreshing thing I've ever had. Suddenly, I'm not in the desert anymore. I'm at a beach party, and there are half–naked women jiggling around me, cheering my name. Then I wake up."

"Hmmm," said Doctor Hank as he scribbled. "And I assume…"

"Yes," Richard said, nodding his double chins. "When I wake up, all I want is Port Mort Kola. I get kegs of it vacuumed to my house now. I had to get a bigger fridge."

Doctor Hank munched on the end of his pen for a few seconds. "This is very serious," he said, clapping his pad shut. "You clearly have a problem with taking responsibility for your actions. You have gained thirty pounds in the past month. You sit around the house swilling soft drinks, but instead of blaming yourself, you blame your dreams. Very serious." He leapt to his feet, and clapped his hands again. Fluorescent light flooded the room once more. The couch tossed Richard to the floor, and deflated. The W.E. walked to a wall console, checked a display screen, and made a few adjustments.

Richard jerked, feeling a stinging in his chest. "What are you doing?" he asked, clutching his chunky breasts.

"I'm reprogramming the heart to compensate for your extra weight, and to keep up with the aerobic regimen I'm going to prescribe."

"What about my nightmares?" Richard asked. He grimaced as his heart surged against his ribs.

Doctor Hank sighed. "I've told you," he said, "the subconscious is a fickle mistress. You have to listen to her. Like it or not, she's the boss." He tapped another section of the display, causing Richard to twitch in synch. "My advice to you is to listen to your dreams. They know what you need to be happy." He gave Richard a few more spasms by remote. "See you next month."

Richard had read once that everyone dreamt three times a night, they just usually did not remember them. Before the accident, he had rarely recalled his dreams. Now he remembered them all in vivid detail.

In his nightmares, an army of reeking sows chased him in the rain, all wanting to have their way with him. He tried to run, but he was too obese, and his shoes just slid in the mud. After a few nights of being amorously pursued by livestock, he bought himself a Tummy Trainer Treadmill, a Sure Stepper, and a decade's supply of Proti–Yum vitamins.

As Richard's physique improved, his nightly horror show worsened. In them, he walked down streets of shining gold, packed with beautiful pedestrians. He, however, was dressed like a derelict. Urine–soaked rags clung to his body. Some nights he was a clown. On the most embarrassing nights he wore nothing at all. The passersby kicked and beat him to the gutter. They all wore Bum–Squeeze Jeans and crew shirts with little goldfish embroidered on them. Somehow, he knew that they would accept him, would care for him, would make passionate love to him, if only he fit in. After two nights, Richard took the hint, and bought himself a designer wardrobe.

Every few weeks, he returned to the Wellness Clinic. Every time, Doctor Hank readjusted his ticker. But no matter what the good W.E. prescribed, the nightmares kept getting worse. Six months to the day of his resurrection, a haggard, trembling Richard Bringham stumbled into the clinic. Doctor Hank pursed his lips as he examined his favorite patient. "What's wrong with you?" he asked. "The last time you were here, we discussed your dreams of a ninety–six inch VirtuViewer. Didn't you buy it? Isn't it keeping you happy?"

"No," Richard said. "No, it isn't." He glared at his Wellness Extraspecialist. "You said to listen to my dreams. The dreams said I needed the VirtuViewer to escape."

Doctor Hank frowned, scratching his chin. "And it's not working?"

"It is, that's the problem," Richard said. "I never wanted to escape before. I never spent my free time watching virts. Now that's all I want to do. What's the point of living if all I want to do is escape?"

"Now, now, now," said Doctor Hank. He gave Richard a fatherly pat on his shoulder. "You've been through a very traumatic experience. It's only natural that your inner voices conflict with each other. Listen to your dreams, for they are the music of your soul."

Richard looked at him with pleading, bloodshot eyes. "Can't you give me something to stop the dreams?" he asked.

"Stop the dreams?" Doctor Hank whispered, his eyes wide. "What are you, insane?" He spun to the wall console, and stabbed at it. "You need the dreams, they are your salvation."

A lightning storm erupted inside of Richard's chest. "Please," he gasped, "can't you just prescribe some sort of sedative?"

"I am prescribing," said Doctor Hank, his face puffy and red. "I am prescribing that you listen to you." He punctuated every syllable with a jab at the touchpad. "You just get a good night's rest, and remember to listen."

The nightly insanity rose to a crescendo.

Richard dreamt of Port Mort Kolas, Follicle Friends, Bum–Squeezes, and VirtuViewers. An army of brand name logos chased him through a maze of streets. When they caught him, they tore off his no–frills cotton t–shirt, and branded his flesh with a red–hot iron that spelled

TRAITOR. "Listen," the logos commanded, drowning out his screams. "Listen!"

He consulted nine different Wellness Extraspecialists. After checking his history, all of them told him to stop whining, and just follow his dreams. None would prescribe anything to stop them. After a month of condescension from reputable W.E.s, Richard decided to seek out a disreputable one.

Of course, taking prescriptions from such a person was illegal. Suffering nightmares alone in his bedroom was one thing, suffering them alongside a cellmate was another. But in the end, it only took a few phone calls and a painful amount of money.

The trail of shady contacts led Richard to an alley that stank of human refuse. He staggered down it, occasionally avoiding bundles of soiled blankets that moved. He shook, certain that she would not show, that he had been set up, that it was all a joke. Just as he was ready to turn and run, a rusty steel door screeched open, and his promised savior lurched forth.

She was sixtyish. Tics randomly cracked her leathery face. She held out a nicotine–stained claw as Richard approached. He hesitated, then dropped a cashier's chit into it. She examined the chit in the amber glow of the streetlights, and shrugged. She reached into her tattered white coat, pulled out a small plastic bottle, and smacked it into Richard's hand. He stared at it, praying he had not just paid a thousand credits for sugar pills, or worse. "Are you sure this is right?" he asked. "I just want to… I need to get some rest." But when he looked up, she was gone.

Richard clutched the bottle to his chest, not daring to release it until he was home. He gulped two of the tranquilizers down dry and curled up on his bed, not bothering to take off his clothes. The pills were not bitter, nor were they sweet. He did not feel dizzy, or nauseous. *My God,* he thought, *they're the real deal.* Tears of relief ran down his cheeks as he sank into darkness, a darkness that was a dreamless bliss.

The funeral, paid for by Americana, was held at an Eternal Rest Crematorium. Doctor Hank stood in the back of the tiny congregation, swaying back and forth to the organ's dirge. He felt obligated to be present. His prize patient had suffered total heart failure. Obviously, there were some problems with the beta–three model. Perhaps they would have better luck with the beta–four.

A tear ran down the Wellness Extraspecialist's cheek as the pearl–encrusted gates of the furnace parted, and Richard's coffin slid inside. He consoled himself that it was not his fault, that his patient should have known better. After all, what kind of fool expected adware to work if he blocked the advertisements?

FALSE IDOLS

Travis unlocked the hatch of his emergency pod, and spun it counterclockwise. A blast of methane shoved him back as the denser atmosphere of Beta Cassiopeiae XII equalized with the air inside. He struggled to his feet, his breath echoing within his helmet. He braced his boots against the hull, and shoved the door as hard as he could, swinging it outward.

A heavy wind carrying tendrils of glowing mist buffeted him, rippling the silver foil of his environment suit. He looked up. On approach, the atmosphere had been clear. Now the sky was a featureless, brown–grey muck. He had only about thirty feet of visibility before the rocks and desert melted into the gloom. He rubbed one of the passing phosphorescent wisps between his fingertips. There was some resistance. The substance clung to his glove for just an instant before floating off. He dropped the pod's chain ladder, and descended to the surface.

His scanner estimated that James had crashed five miles away. Travis oriented himself in what he hoped was the right direction, and began to walk. The eggshell clay under his boots was dense and cracked. Every few minutes, the scanner corrected his course.

"Travis?"

The voice, laced with static, crackled inside his helmet. Travis winced, and adjusted the volume.

"James?" he asked. "James, are you ok?"

There was a pause. Five seconds went by, then ten. Travis wondered if he had suffered some sort of auditory hallucination. He turned the volume back up. He heard quick, jerking sniffs. "James?" he asked.

"I'm sorry," James sobbed through a sea of electronic gibberish. "...Such an idiot, ...ucked everything up."

"It's ok," Travis said. "Where are you now? Can you boost your antenna at all?"

"Do you even know what... means?" James asked. "Lock... frequency at two zero three point nine seven megahertz."

Travis complied. The screeches and intermittent whistling went away. "Can you hear me?" he asked.

"Yes," James said. The software engineer's voice sounded flanged, but his signal was clean. "I hear you."

"Can you help me out with your location?"

There was a pause. "My left leg is broken. I got twisted in my ladder, and fell. I'm not young like you."

"Did your suit puncture?"

"Don't ask stupid questions," James said. "My DualCoder finger is intact. I know that's all you care about."

A faint scuttling sound, like the whisper of a snake's rattle, echoed across the canyon. Travis stopped, and held his breath. All he could hear was the wind.

"Travis?"

"Shush."

He scanned the horizon. He could not make anything out except the clay, the occasional smooth boulder, a few thorny shrubs, and, in the thick of the fog, something that was either a cliff wall, or a steep ridge. The scanner was of no help.

"Travis?"

He let his breath out in a long sigh. "I thought I heard something," he said.

"Just your imagination."

Travis bit the inside of his cheek. "James, I'm sorry I got you into this," he said, marching on once more. "Why did you jump ship?"

"We sinned, Travis. We stole from the Church."

"We found information that can save lives," Travis said. "There's a difference."

He could make out a column of smoke in the distance, just beyond the ridge. He assumed it came from James's pod, and cursed silently. Through occasional clear patches in the billowing miasma, he saw that the sedimentary rock face was at least a hundred feet high, and stretched miles in each direction. More importantly, the pods had atmosphere recyclers, but the suits did not. He only had an hour of air left.

"All the colonies use Invictus Intelligrain," James said. "It is Sol's will. We challenged that will, and now look at us."

"It's poison," said Travis. "It's swimming with toxins, and they know it."

"The digestive systems of the faithful can handle it."

Catherine looked up at him with large, faultless, brown eyes. She was terrified. She had been sick, and her vomit was red. Her whole dress was stained with —

Travis squeezed the memory from his mind. "My daughter has Crimsons," he said. "She's four."

"I'll pray for her."

Travis closed his eyes. "I don't understand," he said. "If you felt this way, why did you help me?"

"You tempted me with money. You lured me away from Sol's light, and into sin."

"Letting millions die isn't a sin?"

Travis could hear James breathing hard. "The Pontifex Maximus knows the will of Sol," the elder man said at last.

Travis checked his scanner. It estimated another one and a half miles to go. That was assuming he would not have to scale the ridge. He cycled the sensors through various spectrums. The luminescent wisps caused too much interference to survey the landscape beyond forty feet, but his scanner had charted his course as he walked. He looked at the map, and swallowed.

About a fifth of a mile back, he had been walking on a road.

"Travis?" James asked. "Travis, can you hear me?"

Travis switched the radio off, and considered his options. The most important factor was air, and the direct route was usually best. However, a road was some sort of construction, and there was a good possibility that it led to a passage.

Travis retraced his steps to the road, and wondered how he had missed it. It was much harder beneath his feet than the clay that made up the rest of the landscape. He knelt, and brushed at the top layer. The surface underneath was dark, and mirror–polished. He ignited his arc knife, and tried to cut a piece off. The blue–white line of plasma flared against the murky glass, but left it unscathed. He pocketed the tool, and switched his radio back on. "Are you still there?" he asked.

"I'm still here," James said. "You hung up on me. Do not ever —"

"Shut up," Travis cut him off. "I found a road." There were a few moments of silence. "Do you hear me, jackass?"

"I hear you."

"There's intelligent life on this planet, or at least there was. Contamination is an executable sin."

"So is stealing from the Church."

Travis pressed his forehead against the cool glass of his faceplate. "I have friends," he said. "They could have helped us. Now we'll never get out of here. I know you were scared, but what the hell were you thinking?"

"Well, you didn't have to follow me." James began to cry again. "I am a sinner, and the light of Sol Invictus will protect me in all things," he chanted. "I am a sinner, and the light of Sol —"

Travis snapped the radio off. He had two choices: return to the pod, set the beacon, put himself in suspended animation, and claim ignorance if rescue ever arrived — or move forward, and find James.

Catherine — just her name was enough. He did not want to recall her bloody image again. He had to find James, and retrieve his half of the data. Besides, he realized as he checked his tank, in forty–five minutes he would have to return to the pod anyway.

He whipped his head around. He could have sworn he heard the whispering rattle again, but he saw nothing. He took a deep breath, and headed down the road.

A pair of objects appeared on the scanner as flat planes within the ridge's wall. Travis was not sure what they were at first, but as he got closer, he saw that they were gates. Each side was ten feet high, and twenty feet wide. What he took initially to be wrought iron filigree was in fact a network of twisted vines. He pulled at them. They were as hard as steel. He put his gloves where the two monstrous gates joined, and pushed with all of his strength. They refused to budge.

He stepped back, and examined the interwoven design. He decided that it might be possible to cut a hole large enough to crawl through. He ignited his knife.

The vines lashed out the moment the fire touched them. Travis jerked back, dropping his knife to the road, but he was not fast enough. They whipped around the fingertips of his right hand, and constricted. He screamed as the bones in his middle, ring, and index fingertips snapped, popping in rapid succession like firecrackers. He yanked back his mutilated hand, but the vines squeezed harder. With a wrenching twist, they tore off his fingertips.

Agony exploded up Travis's arm. He fell back to the ground, dimly aware of the whoosh of escaping oxygen. There was a new pain now as the suit clamped around his fingers at their first joints. He felt a prick in his wrist, and his hand went blessedly numb. White fire flared around his knuckles, and he watched as the remaining halves of his three torn fingers plopped one by one to the crystalline road. The glove twisted itself tight at the end of his stubs, like sausage casing. The whooshing noise stopped.

"Attention," a pleasant female voice said in his ear. "Your Aurelian–Award environment suit has detected a breach, and possible biological contaminants. Contaminated digits have been amputated, and the relevant breaches sealed. Please seek immediate medical assistance. Aurelian–Award apologizes for any inconvenience."

Travis lay sprawled on the ground, staring at what was left of his hand. The vines still clutched his fingertips, and the torn silver swatches of his glove. The bioluminescent fog descended upon the discarded digits. There was a sound like the drone of angry hornets, and then the glowing wisps dissipated.

What were once his fingertips were now amber crystals streaked with flaws the color of cinnamon. Every detail had been transformed. He could make out the whorls on their undersides, the cracked nails, the hardened veins sticking out like yellow, glistening wires amidst the torn joints, and even the bones underneath.

The vines tossed his crystallized fingers and their silvery wrappings to the ground. They reached for him, extending two feet out of their filigree. Travis scuttled in the dust, pushing himself to his feet with his one good hand. The vines stretched as far as they could in his direction. Then, with a creaking groan, the gates inched apart.

Travis darted back, clamping his mutilated hand underneath his armpit. The gates screeched outward, the vines swirling toward him like snakes. He watched as the gap widened to a foot, then two, and then three.

He ran.

The razor–sharp tip of a vine scraped a furrow across his faceplate as he passed between them. The hinges screeched as the gate fought its own momentum, and switched directions. He continued running, his feet pounding on the hardened clay. He turned his head to see the gate swing shut behind him with a reverberating clang. His foot caught on a rock, and he sprawled forward.

He lifted his head. It was not a rock, it was a root. He reached out for the tree, and pulled himself to his feet. Then he realized it was not a tree, and what he had tripped over was not a root.

It was a tentacle.

The statue was seven feet high. Its face, if Travis could call it that, was a mass of segmented eyes at its center. It was fashioned from the same crystal as the road and his amputated fingers, but it had a bluish hue, as if carved from a cloudy sapphire. Its seven tentacles each ended in a maw lined with needles. Circling the eyes were three rows of overlapping ridges. Beneath the ridges, Travis could make out a silvery hose that led to some mechanism deep within its chest.

Travis stared at the sculpture, his breath coming in long, hard gasps. He swallowed back nausea. Three fingers. He had lost three fingers because of James's stupidity, on his right hand, no less. Praise Invictus he had not lost his pinky. He wiggled his remaining digits. They obeyed. His hand no longer felt numb and it did not hurt, but holy shit, did it itch. He rubbed his stumps with the thumb of his left glove. "Warning," the suit's voice said in his ear, "please do not agitate the emergency seal, or temporary grafting epoxy. Seek immediate medical attention. Aurelian–Award apologizes for any inconvenience."

Travis cried out in frustration and rage. It would have been worth it if he could have saved Catherine.

At the foot of the statue was an obsidian table, about two feet high, in the shape of an ankh. Runes adorned every inch of its surface. The round head was shaped like a shallow bowl. The depression was riddled with holes, as if it had been jackhammered with a spike. Each of the three spokes bore nests of vines. Travis stepped back from them. There was a brackish residue along the center of the cross's arms and length. The luminescent wisps floating about Travis's head made something shiny glint at the center of the depression. He picked it up.

It was hard, clear, and irregular, like bubbled glass. It was curved, a shard of a sphere, with a spiderweb crack radiating from its center. A stringy, opaque, green and gold material clung to its surface, dangling a network of what looked like veins and nerves. Travis held it up to the horizon. He could make out the pillar of smoke through it, barely visible through the fog.

He heard a rustling noise from behind him. He half turned as something exploded into the back of his knee. He fell, cracking his other knee on the corner of the altar. He rolled onto the clay as the vines on the cross's arms lashed out for him.

A man in an environment suit stepped between Travis and the sky, aiming a flare gun at his stomach. Travis squinted. Through the reflected landscape in the faceplate, he could make out ice–blue eyes peering down at him from a somber, wrinkled face.

His helmet speaker snapped on with a click. "Very slowly," James said in a cold, commanding voice, "remove your knife, and toss it over."

Travis held up his mutilated hand. "I lost it when this happened," he said.

"When what happened?"

Travis stared up at James, aware of the vines attached to the altar flexing just at the edge of his vision. "I tried to cut a sample of the road, and it exploded," he said. "There was some sort of resonance feedback from the crystal."

James tilted his head, considering. "I'm not sure if I believe you," he said, "but it doesn't matter. Hold your hand out."

Travis extended his right hand. James opened his pouch, removed a DualCoder, and laid it on the clay. He knelt on one knee, his flare gun steady, his eyes never leaving Travis's. He slipped his pinky inside. There was a chirp, and his end of the device lit up with a red glow.

"Now you," he instructed.

"Answers first."

James's face remained expressionless. "I can still make your finger work after you're dead," he said. "It's not as difficult as the advertising claims."

Travis bit his lip, and pushed his finger inside. He felt a tingle, like static electricity. His end of the device lit up blue. At the center of the DualCoder the colors swirled, forming fractal patterns. They merged into a violet ring, and the device emitted a high, satisfied chord. James yanked it off Travis's finger, and stood. He pressed a button, and a chip the size of his fingernail popped out. He removed it, and placed it in his pouch.

"Thank you Travis," James said. "The secrets of Intelligrain will be the icing on the cake."

Panic bloomed in Travis's chest. "Who do you work for?" he asked.

"Don't be cliché," said James. "Does it matter? All the religions are fighting over colonization rights. The Vatican, Hunahpu City, the Pontifex Maximus, the Synod, the Caliphate… everybody wants a piece of this planet."

The pulse in Travis's temples began to throb. "There's intelligent life here," he said. "We're contaminators. No one would ever think of rescuing you now, no matter what you've discovered."

The elder man gestured to the statue. "This planet's already been contaminated," he said. "Look at the ridges around the eyes. What does that tell you?"

"Insomnia?"

"If you had only bothered to look," James continued, "you would have seen that every organ, vein, bone, and muscle have been crystalized. Those ridges are gills. There seems to be some sort of artificial breathing mechanism grafted inside. Apparently, non–biological material isn't affected by the process."

Travis shrugged.

"Gills, you idiot, on a world without an ocean. At least one other race made it to this planet before us, which makes the contamination charge invalid. The problem was that we needed a way to accidentally 'discover' that. And then you came along with your crusade, looking for a hacker, and promising espionage of Intelligrain intel from a ship on the Cassiopeiae run no less. How could we pass it up?"

"What the hell are you talking about?" Travis asked.

James let out a weary sigh. "Survey probes suggested months ago that this planet has some very unique life–forms. The natives are some sort of microscopic insects. They can chew material up and spit it out with molecular detail, like bees masticating honey into wax. But this wax has a crystalline structure more perfect than a diamond's."

"Imagine that, bugs that can transubstantiate."

James glowered at him. "Imagine if we exposed certain biological forms to them," he said, "if we genetically engineered animal life in the exact shapes needed for light–phase hyperdrive crystals." He held his arms out. "This world will become the center of the galaxy. And it will be under our… guidance." He stepped back, and leveled the flare gun at Travis's chest. "This may sting a little."

"Wait," Travis said, holding his hands out. "What about my daughter?"

James gave him a look that was almost pity. "Don't you get it?" he asked. "Nobody gives a shit about Crimsons. Do you think that's the only disease Intelligrain causes? Who cares, it makes colonization possible." He clicked his tongue. "Besides, when has theology ever been a friend of knowledge? Adam and Eve were cast from paradise for wanting to think for themselves. For bringing mortals the gift of fire, Prometheus was damned to have his organs be eagle chow for all eternity. For daring to teach that the Earth was not the center of creation, Galileo was imprisoned. The other religions don't want to bring Sol Invictus down, they just want their cut."

Travis nodded at the altar. "It won't be perfect though," he said. "There's some organic matter there. How come it hasn't been transformed?"

James's eyes narrowed. Almost involuntarily, they flicked to the polished ankh.

Travis kicked upward into James's stomach. The engineer fired as he fell, burning a path through the air millimeters from Travis's faceplate. Travis staggered, blinded. He squeezed his eyes tight against the pain, waiting for the killing shot.

Seconds passed. He opened his eyes, and blinked through the dying after–glare.

James had fallen onto the ankh. The vines wrapped around his shoulder and neck, pulling him against the altar in an iron grasp, the flare gun still clenched in his hand. Obeying an unheard command, a wind blew across the wasteland, pushing the dank fog back to the horizon. Only the glowing wisps remained.

Beneath the glistening band of the Milky Way, the landscape was littered with statues, altars, shards of green glass, and about a hundred yards away, the smoking wreckage of James's pod. Travis recognized some of the species that made up the idols. There were creatures from Centauri and Betelgeuse, even a five–winged avian from AD Leonis. The rest were life forms he had never seen before. There was one he could only describe as a hybrid between a wasp, a squid, and a horse.

The ground shook with a low rumble, like an earthquake. James strained and squirmed to raise his head. "Travis?" he shouted. "What's happening?"

They came from everywhere, from holes in the rocks, from the mountains, and from the cliffs. They were insectile, their exoskeletons sporting three spindly legs and an armored abdomen. Their twisted necks ended in one milky eye that looked as if it was made of glass, with an opal fluid sloshing inside. Their irises were uniformly the color of cinnamon, flecked with streaks of scarlet. There were hundreds of thousands of them, all roughly two feet high. They chattered and whispered as they came.

Travis tore open James's pouch. He snatched the data chip, and dropped it into his own. A moment later, the sea of insects flowed around him, pushing him back from the altar.

He did not resist. An eerie calm settled over him. Whatever happened next, he had no defense. They swarmed over James's struggling form, and wrapped their cursorial legs around him. The vines retracted as the insects yanked their prey to his feet.

The glowing wisps of fog descended, and enveloped the engineer's helmet. There was a flash of orange and white as James fired into the onslaught. A handful of creatures ignited, their charred bodies spinning through the air. Finally, one shimmied up James's suit, and smashed his faceplate with its foreleg. He screamed as the phosphorescence assaulted his mouth and nostrils. He writhed, his hands tearing at his crystallizing throat. The insects dug their razor–tipped claws into his environment suit, shredding it from his body. They could not scratch his flesh, as it was now a hardened, emerald resin.

The naked statue glinted in the starlight, his arms thrown upward, his legs twisted. His mouth was a grimace of agony, his sagging paunch hanging over shriveled genitalia. Through the clear green crystal of James's clenched pinky, Travis could make out his DualCoder key implant. And there, in his mouth, were the glints of fillings. The swarm stood in reverent silence now, their rattling nothing more than a light rustle.

They were waiting.

A piercing, high–pitched cry pealed across the winds. The sea of brown–eyed insects parted, forming a path to the altar. Two of them dragged a third, gibbering and screaming, to the stone table. They threw it down, where it fought until the vines held fast its thrashing limbs.

Its eye was green.

A cinnamon–eyed insect, larger than the others, mounted the wretched supplicant. It loomed above its captive, slowly rearing back on two hind legs, its foreleg quivering in the air. It looked upward to its new idol for guidance. Then it lunged, driving its claw into the sacrifice's pupil.

Its emerald eye shattered, drenching James's agonized statue and the surrounding congregation in viscous, opal fluid. A cloud of luminescent vapor rose from the shards, and became one with the formation of glowing wisps. The anointed ones waved their middle legs in the air, chattering in ecstasy as the poor, impaled creature writhed, and then fell still.

Travis ran.

The insects either did not notice, or, in their rapture, did not care. He raced to James's pod, his breath like fire in his lungs.

"Your oxygen is depleted," the suit's voice said pleasantly. "Please lie down, and meditate until help arrives. Estimated time to unconsciousness is ten minutes."

Travis pulled himself up the chain ladder. The army of insects approached. They did not run; they knew there was nowhere he could go. He pulled the handle, and twisted it.

The round door swung outwards, but there was no hiss of pressurization. Travis gritted his teeth. The insects were at the foot of the ladder now. He swung the door closed behind him, and locked it.

"Computer," he said, "what's the status of the pod?"

"Linking," the voice said in his ear. "Oxygen refinery damaged upon impact."

Travis tore through the lockers of survival gear until he found a data transmitter. It was the size of his thumb. He pulled the chip from his pouch, and snapped it inside.

The sound of claws beating against the door was like hail. "Analysis of crystal structures outside?" he asked.

There was a pause. "Transparent, yet extremely dense atomic mesh," the suit said, "unbreakable to known technology."

Travis nodded. "I want the information on this chip broadcast continuously," he said.

"The transmitter will need direct sunlight every thirty–five point two hours to recharge."

"What is the daylight cycle of this planet?"

"Twenty–six hours."

The pod rocked back and forth. Travis had no doubt the insects would soon find their way inside. "'This world will become the center of the galaxy,'" he quoted. "I'm going to open my faceplate. Can you seal my suit at the neck?"

"Safety protocols —"

"Override," he said. "Trap what air you can inside my suit below my neck until my faceplate is sealed again. Then flush the atmosphere from my helmet, and release." There was a pause. "Do it."

He felt a tightening around his neck. "Suit sealed." The voice was almost resentful.

He took a deep breath, held it, and swung his faceplate open. Keeping his throat clenched, he opened his mouth enough to slip the transmitter inside. His lungs burned. He smacked the faceplate closed. There was a hiss as the suit cleared his helmet, and the pressure drop made his eyes feel as if they were going to pop from his skull. Then the squeezing around his neck released, and he sucked sour air in through his teeth.

"Time to unconsciousness recalculated due to available oxygen and accelerated heartbeat. Now only three point four minutes remaining."

"One more thing," he slurred around the object in his mouth. "Pump my body full of local anesthetic."

"I am only authorized to do that in case of injury."

"I'll be dead in less than four minutes, I promise not to tell anyone," he said. "Please?"

There was a pause, and then a jabbing sensation. After a few seconds, he could only feel numbness.

"Anesthetic administered."

With a metallic screech, the insects tore the hatch from its hinges. *Wait,* Travis begged silently, *not here!* As if they could hear his thoughts, the creatures wrapped their spider–like legs around his arms, and yanked him outside, dragging him down the ladder to the clay.

He pushed himself to his feet. An altar had been constructed at the base of the pod, with a trembling, green–eyed sacrifice already in waiting. The insects pushed Travis forward. He did not resist. Although he could not feel it, he could hear the transmitter buzzing against his teeth. He clenched his lips together. For Catherine, he would protect it. *I love you,* he thought. Was there a way of transmitting that as well?

The glowing fog descended. As a claw smashed his faceplate, he puffed his chest out, and inhaled the wisps through his nose. If he was to be the universe's first god of knowledge, he decided, he would be a god that was proud.

He gazed down on his poor sacrifice, and, as his final act, forced his crystalizing lips into a smile.

THE ARENA

"Egg chutes me please, human?"

An Oligochaetan family loomed over me. They had amassed themselves into a gestalt humanoid form. It weaved its wormy head from side to side as its mouth squirmed to form the words.

"Do you mean 'excuse me?'" I asked.

"Yes, please, our English is still in–perk–fact. We wish to sit here, in the affront. It is in the shades, and will keep us cool and safe from your nasty, fakery sun."

That was not good. While there were private lounges upstairs, arena seats were sold on a first–come, first–served basis, and I had been there first. However, Oligochaetans were an endangered species, and by law were to be given every courtesy. I needed to sit in the front, but I also needed to not draw attention to that fact. I stood. "What are the odds today?" I asked.

The conglomeration drew back its misshapen head in feigned surprise. "Oh human," it said, "we would not stink to such low, illegritimate gambling on such a fine day."

I snorted. It was no secret that the Iweala family owned all the gambling dens on Ganymede, the arena, the Flopper, and my brother. "How much?" I asked.

It darted its crafted eyes from side to side. "Five to one that Abran gives the Flopper death within four blows," it said in a voice throaty and warbling. "He is not gruel."

It took me a moment to understand. "No," I agreed, "he is not."

I relinquished my seat. The mass of worms poured into it, spilling through the gap in the back before reforming. I wondered if they would lose their coherence when they, along with the rest of the crowd, lost their bets.

It would be a fair fight.

I gazed into a sky half–filled by Jupiter and a handful of its other moons. The rest were blotted out by the glare of JOV–7. Naturalists had protested against terraforming Ganymede, but it turned out alien species were much more adaptable than we were. They were also much less prone to moral outrage. A blind eye was turned in the outer colonies to many things Earth deemed illegal. The arena was one of them, and Abran was very much a part of it.

I stopped climbing. My thoughts had taken me halfway into the stadium, and I needed to be close to the ring. The problem was that there were no seats available below the twentieth row. I looked at my watch. We had fourteen minutes to go. What the hell, I decided as I took a vacant seat by the stairs, I could run.

"Well, Heitor, this is a surprise," purred an alto voice, thick and sweet. "What are you doing up here in the cheap seats?" A hologram flickered into life in the seat next to mine. It was of an elegant woman in her mid–fifties, with piercing eyes the color of midnight. She wore a red dress, and sat with her legs crossed through the seat in front of her. I assumed from her posture that she was in her private lounge, relaxing on a settee. I turned, looked up at her tinted windows, and waved.

"Good afternoon, Adeola," I said. "Fancy meeting you here."

Adeola Iweala grinned, displaying two rows of perfect, bleached teeth. "Heitor, Heitor, Heitor. I hear you're going back to Earth tonight. Don't you like it here on our little colony?" I opened my mouth to reply, but she continued. "The funny thing is, your brother never mentioned it to me. Isn't that funny?"

"Hilarious."

Adeola chuckled. "Don't be cute with me, Heitor," she said, her deep voice soft and friendly. "It would only take a word to have you found in the morning with your throat and testicles slit." I felt a static electric tickle as she caressed my cheek with the back of her lacquered fingernails. "Why won't you work for me? Abran does well, doesn't he?"

He hates you, I thought. *Worse than that, you've made him hate himself.* "There's a lot of good work back on Earth," I said.

"True," she agreed, "unskilled monkeys can find jobs anywhere. But what really interests me is that you've chartered a private transport with twenty–three hundred pounds of cargo space. That must have been expensive. Much cheaper to sell your belongings and start fresh, yes?"

Something tightened inside of my chest. "My furniture has a lot of sentimental value," I said at last.

"That's sweet," said Adeola. "Maybe I'll have my boys help you move it. You must be packed by now, right?" I didn't reply. She took a sip of something red from a crystal glass. "Are you going to come back and visit Abran and me?" she asked. "He's going to miss you." I remained silent. She sniffed. "I took his shitty little roadside attraction, and made it the greatest show in the outer planets. It was to settle your gambling debts, if I recall. Aren't you grateful?"

I thought of how my brother drank almost every night just to sleep. He could wire the poor creature to only mimic pain and death, but Adeola had insisted that he program it to feel the real thing — because suffering was what people paid to see. I thought of his face week after week as he smashed through the Flopper's clockworks and bellows to the crowd's thunderous applause, of the creature screaming and clawing at its wounds as its gears, wires, and pneumatic fluid erupted from its sides. When Abran delivered the killing blow, his jaw would clench and the cords in his neck would tighten, but only I could recognize the shame in his eyes. And then, throughout the week, he would resurrect his creation. His hands would stroke its aluminum flanks, and polish its lenses and brass finish, only to torture and murder it again come Saturday night.

"Thank you," I said.

Adeola sniffed. "Very good," she said. She squeezed my thigh, her long, exquisite fingers passing through it. "Send me a post card when you get to Earth. I have some friends there. Maybe they'll find work for a pretty boy like you."

The band's overture echoed across the arena. "Maybe," I said.

Adeola clicked her tongue. Before she could reply, the blanket jammer switched on, and her hologram fizzled out. I checked my watch. The fight had started late. We had less than ten minutes.

The crowd roared as a man in his late twenties strode into the ring, his scarlet cape fluttering behind him, his gauntlet clenched about his left fist. The thirty–foot–high screens circling the arena focused on his worn features: his lined mouth, his dark, hollow eyes. I hoped that I was the only one who could see the fear behind his concentration. He turned his stolid expression from left to right as the audience cheered, and pounded their feet. Then he saw the Oligochaetans sitting in my usual seat, and flinched. I knew he could not see me so far back, not with the floodlights in his eyes. It did not matter. The plan was in motion, and nothing could stop it.

The glorious mechanical demon was released, its roar like a knife through my eardrums. It raced onto the field, the pounding of its steel hooves shaking the stadium. Jets of orange fire thrust it a few feet into the sky, just enough to tower over the matador. It swiveled its one glowing eye to focus on him, its pupil swirling down to a pinprick. It roared again.

My brother bowed to it, a fencer saluting his opponent. He unhooked his cape, and swung it from his neck. With the whirring of pistons and gears, the Flopper reared back, and raised its arm. There was the smell of ozone and burning copper as its claw ignited with forks of lightning. Abran leapt to the side, swirling his cape through the air. The thunderbolt burned a flaming path through it. The crowd screamed and applauded. I checked my watch. There were six minutes to go.

My brother taunted the beast again and again with his flowing scarlet promise of insanity, pain, and death. The creature lowered itself to the earth and charged, its barbed horn aimed for Abran's stomach. He dove to the side, and punched the creature's flank with his titanium gauntlet. The charges in the knuckles exploded into the Flopper's armor, cracking a plate open. It screamed, its great eye rolling back in its clockwork skull. The crowd cheered and stomped their feet as the screens zoomed in on the creature's agony, a creature who had once given rides to laughing children at carnivals.

I looked at my watch again. I had two minutes. The blanket field jammed transmissions within the audience, but Abran said my watch would work if I was inside the ring. I eyed the stairs, but if Adeola saw me run down them now, she would be suspicious.

The Flopper lunged again, and my brother spun to one side, as graceful as a danseur. He punched the same armor plate he had cracked before, his gauntlet tearing into the beast's innards. Gears slipped, and ground together with a metallic screech. I had twenty–two seconds.

The Flopper reared up on its jets, its claw crackling with forks of blue–white fire. My brother raised his scorched, tattered cape, and leaned to the side to parry.

My watch ran down to zero.

Lightning exploded from the claw, washing over my brother. I rose with the crowd as his broken body twisted through the air, and fell to the earth. Everything — the spectators, the noise, the Flopper — seemed to slow down. I lunged down the steps, my feet pounding on the concrete. Someone grabbed for me, but I dodged his well–meaning hands, almost sprawling on my face.

I reached the wall at the end of the front row, and leaned forward to hurdle it. Entering the ring during a fight was a felony, but surely the madness of a grieving brother would be forgiven. All that mattered was that the signal from my watch reached the Flopper before security got their bearings, or worse, before it finished Abran off. It roared in triumph as I jumped.

A squirming rope whipped around my waist and yanked me back, jerking the breath out of me. I looked down. The Oligochaetans had lassoed me, their bodies woven into an elongated serpent. They anchored one end around their seat, the other around me.

"Let me go!" I shouted as I tore at their wormy bodies, my fingers slipping in–between them.

"Be at peas," the gestalt said, its mouth pointing up at me. "You can't kelp now."

I stretched my arm as far as I could into the arena, aiming my watch at the Flopper. *Download the release code,* I screamed inside. *Download, and fly into orbit —*

There was a whistle, followed by a thunderclap. The lower half of the Flopper's head exploded, showering down a rain of gears and pneumatic fluid. Its jaw hung, cockeyed, its rows of needle–sharp teeth scraping its neck. Its eye rolled in its swivels, the iris swirling open and closed.

The security team fired again, and this time the Flopper's body burst into flames, its oil igniting. Its jets fired, and it hovered in the air for a second, its twisted steel frame dangling its shattered head backwards. Then it fell to the dirt.

I slumped against the wall as the worms uncoiled from my waist. The on–site paramedics attended to my brother. They raised him onto a stretcher, and ran him off the field. I made my way down to the gate in a daze. The security team recognized me, and escorted me through.

By the time I reached the arena's infirmary, Abran had already been pronounced dead. He lay on a stretcher, covered by a sheet. I pulled it back to see my brother's face. He did not look peaceful.

A lieutenant from the local garrison stood over my shoulder, making notes on his data pad. He scratched his bald head behind his ear. "Are you still planning to return to Earth this evening?" he asked.

I nodded. "Can I take his body with me?" I asked.

The lieutenant shrugged. Though expensive, it was not unheard of for the remains of colonists to be returned to Earth. And though he did not know it, I had already paid more than ten times necessary in freight. There was no need for an autopsy. Abran had been electrocuted in front of ten thousand eyewitnesses. What else was there to know?

The clack of heels echoed from the hallway. The doors flew open and Adeola stormed into the infirmary, flanked by her two sons. One, a colossal figure with triceps like tree trunks, took a spot by the door. The other stayed a respectful two steps behind her.

"Excuse me, ma'am," the lieutenant said. "You can't come in here right —"

"Shut up," Adeola said, not bothering to look at him. She yanked my brother's sheet off. She pulled his eyelids back, and stared into his sightless pupils. She whirled on me.

"You," she said. "You and your brother are coming with me."

I looked at the lieutenant. He sighed. "Ma'am, I'm going to have to ask you to leave," he said.

She ignored him. "Are you coming on your own, or are you going to be on the stretcher with him?" she asked me.

"All right, that's enough," said the lieutenant. He tapped a button on his wristwatch, his eyes meeting Adeola's imperial gaze. The doors opened and two corporals came in, their sidearms in hand.

Adeola's right eye twitched. "Are you really fooled by this?" she asked. She slapped my brother's cheek. "I can name at least three drugs that can simulate death for hours. Put one of those in a nano–capsule, and you can time the release down to the quarter–second." She slapped him again. "Those lightning bolts weren't lethal. Do you think I would risk my property like that? His cape is lined with flash powder." She grabbed the charred cloth from my brother's side, and shoved it under the lieutenant's nose. "Smell the sulfur," she said, her voice a low growl.

The lieutenant rolled his eyes. "Call for an ambulance," he said, "and escort Mister Pena and his brother to the shuttle port. See that they get on their transport safely."

Adeola took a deep breath. She walked towards the door, taking long, graceful strides. She stopped, and peered into my face. She said nothing, then stalked out of the medical center, her sons in tow.

An hour later, Abran and I were off into Ganymede's artificial atmosphere. My brother's casket had been secured in the cargo bay. He lay inside, wrapped in a heated blanket. I sat next to him, staring out the porthole as the moon fell away beneath us, a medical kit on my lap.

My watch beeped.

Abran's face twitched. His eyes snapped open, and he gasped.

"Give it a minute," I said. "You may need an adrenaline shot, but I don't want to give it to you if I don't have to."

"Ice," Abran moaned. He clamped his hands to his head. "Jesus Christ, it feels like my brain is full of ice. Give me some hot water, or something." I went to the corridor, and filled a cup from the dispenser. The intercom came on.

"Is he awake?"

"Yes," I said.

"Sorry about your wasted cargo fee," said the pilot. "Tell you what, I'll give you a fifty percent refund."

"Thanks," I said.

"We'll be clearing the Jovian well in another hour. Do you think your brother will be ready to go back under?"

"I don't know."

I headed back inside the cargo bay with the cup of hot water. Abran stood at the porthole, the glowing orange blanket draped over his shoulders. The swirling storms of Jupiter's red spot filled the view.

"We're past the orbital pickup point," Abran said without turning around, "and the Flopper isn't here."

I put the cup in his hand.

"What happened?" he asked.

I told him of the Oligochaetans, of Adeola, and of my failure. "I'm sorry," I said.

"Don't be," said Abran. He turned and smiled at me as he placed his trembling hand on my shoulder. It felt like ice. He sipped the hot water gingerly.

"It's better off dead," he said. "Better off in pieces too small for that bitch to put together again." He finished the water, crushed the paper cup, and let it fall to the floor. "I just wanted to set it free."

I rubbed his back in a half–hug. "We should get ready for the sleep tanks," I said. "It's going to be a very long flight." He nodded, and we walked together towards the door, towards Earth, and towards a new life.

ALL PART OF BEING A DRAGON

Theresa perched on her partner's shoulder as the E train rocked them back and forth. She watched the muscles in his cheek twitch. She hoped he was not sinking into one of his moods again; he was a pain in the ass when he was introspective. If only she was a Dragon, she mused, she would be done with these shitty assignments. "Azrael," she whispered in his ear, "what's wrong with you?"

He did not look at her. He faced straight ahead, his eyes inscrutable behind his mirrored sunglasses. "I hate New York City in this century," he said. "I hate its public transportation. It's not the filth, it's not the rats that crawl onto the tracks, it's not even the vagrants who release enough diseased particles to fuel a biological weapons stockpile." The corners of his mouth descended. "It's the damned inefficiency. Trains that never run on time, tunnels that easily flood, incompetent management…"

"Careful, Mister Sunshine," Theresa said, her forked tongue tickling his neck, "I can smell your indignation circuits sizzling." She slipped her tail inside his ear. "Want me to release some endorphins?"

"Stop that," he said as the E train jerked along its tracks. "Just keep your eyes open."

Theresa jabbed his eardrum with her tail. "Ingrate," she said.

"Hey, it's the Chameleon Man!"

Azrael raised his right eyebrow. The man approaching them was short and plump. He wore a black tracksuit and hot pink boots. Bloodshot eyes leered at them from beneath a leather cap. "Yeah, I read about you in *The Voice,* the man with the giant chameleon. What is it, a puppet?"

Azrael did not answer. He merely stood, his head cocked at a five degree angle.

The man in the pink boots shifted uncomfortably under the disapproving gaze. His eyes shifted from Azrael to Theresa. Theresa flicked her tongue at him. "Yeah, whatever, dick. Yo," he shouted as he slid the between–cars door aside and stepped through, "Chameleon Man's a dick!"

"He's got a point," Theresa said after the door closed. "If they're talking about us in the newspapers, we've lost our advantage. I told you, I should be invisible. Dragons can do that, you know."

"I have no other lead on X–Fifty–Nine except that he is in this miserable city," Azrael said. "He is not one to sit back and bide his time. He will know who we are, and that we are looking for him. He will reach his usual conclusion that the best defense is a good offense, and come after us."

"We've been here three weeks now."

"Patience."

Theresa flicked his earlobe with her tongue. "I could help you find him a lot easier if I was upgraded to Dragon," she said.

His cheek twitched again. "Stop saying that," he said. "You have a good soul. You are perfect just the way you are."

Theresa puffed her neck. His argument always came back to the same place: that she was somehow at fault, somehow not true to herself for wanting more. "You're just worried I'll have more options than your ugly face," she said.

"Quiet."

The train stopped, and its doors opened. A bald man boarded the car, stooping to get his enormous frame inside. He was a sinewy giant, his angular frame concealed by an impeccable navy cloak. His clear, pewter gaze fell upon

Azrael. A grin split his features as his eyes opened wide.

"A. Z. Re–Al," the man said, purring each syllable in a basso profondo that rattled the car's windows. Azrael jerked his head in the voice's direction.

Theresa jammed her tail into Azrael's ear. "Let's do this," she said, activating her half of the sync. A second passed, but Azrael's brain did not reply. "Azrael?" she asked. "Come on, I can't engage containment by myself."

"X–Fifty–Nine," Azrael said as he reached into his tattered trench coat and pulled out a pistol. The passengers screamed, and dropped to the floor.

"Holy shit," Theresa said. "What are you doing?"

"Plague this Tapestry no more," said Azrael, and pumped the trigger.

The gun thundered twice, its shots ricocheting off a pole inches from X–Fifty–Nine's head. Azrael fired again, but instead of a third shot ringing out, an umbrella fluttered open in his hand. He cursed.

X–Fifty–Nine laughed from deep within his belly. He threw his cloak off his shoulders. He stood naked, one hand wielding a carving knife. Its blade was a foot long, and glistened like silver. The other fist gripped a trembling chicken by its scrawny neck. Theresa saw terror in its beady, black eyes, and her stomach sank.

"Don't!" she cried.

X–Fifty–Nine held the chicken and the knife high above his head, touching the car's ceiling. He slashed across the fowl's brown neck. Blood gushed forth. He pirouetted on his callused toes, spraying the cowering passengers in scarlet.

The anointed commuters shrank and writhed. Their noses elongated, and hardened into beaks. Feathers pierced through their skins, and bloomed. Within a minute, the car was occupied by chickens. They crawled from underneath their clothing, and turned their squinting eyes upon Azrael and Theresa.

X–Fifty–Nine laughed again, deep, rich, and echoing. Azrael took slow, deliberate steps backward until he was against the car's side. The chickens leaned forward, opened their razor–sharp beaks, and clucked in unison.

Theresa pushed her tail deeper into Azrael's ear. She tried again to link with him, but there was no response. "What the hell is wrong with you?" she asked. Her skin darkened. She dug her toenails into his shoulder, tearing his coat. "Azrael!" Her partner said nothing, his face a grim statue.

The army of fowl advanced.

Azrael brandished his umbrella, and swung at them in broad arcs. One reached his leg, and dug its beak into his shin. Gritting his teeth against the pain, he drove the umbrella down. It was too blunt to pierce the bird's flesh, but it snapped the creature's ribcage. The chicken let out one final, desperate cluck, and expired.

Its comrades paused, and looked at each other. As if having reached some silent decision, they resumed their attack. They dug their beaks into Azrael's leather boots. He stumbled, tripped over the edge of a seat, and sprawled to the floor, Theresa still clinging to his shoulder.

The feathered army dove upon them.

Theresa hissed, and snapped at the creatures as they stabbed at her. One towered over her, cocked its head, and lunged for her eyes. Azrael's hand shot down at the last second, and covered her face. The bird speared it instead, lodging its beak just below his wrist. He roared in pain, ripped the chicken away, and threw it across the train.

Azrael tore his coat off and wrapped it around Theresa, her scaly face peeking out of its folds. He stood, ignoring the barrage at his back and sides. He spun, and kicked the car's window. It cracked. A second kick, and it shattered. He wrapped his arms around Theresa, and dove through.

He tumbled onto the tracks and rolled, his head stopping just short of the electrified third rail. His arms, back, and legs were lacerated. Theresa could see his left femur poking out against his pants. His hand was a mess of blood, shattered bones, and tendons. He stumbled across the tracks, through the support beams, and to the Manhattan–bound side of the tunnel. He made his way to a service alcove and crouched, clutching Theresa to his chest.

"Azrael," she said, "let me out of here."

"Shush."

"I can't breathe."

Azrael loosened the coat around her mouth. "Thank you," she said. "What the hell are you doing? Why didn't you —"

"Shush."

"Don't shush me, asshole. Why —"

He covered her mouth with his coat again.

The sound of clucking came down the tunnel: agonized, bewildered clucks. Theresa could make out the army of approaching fowl by the dim, blue service lights. "They followed us through the window and regrouped," Azrael said, his voice soft. "Now, will you please shut the hell up?"

Theresa stopped thrashing. She extended her tail, and brushed it against his ear. "Not now," he said. "I'm trying to protect you. Please, just stay still."

Theresa's eyes adjusted to the near darkness. The chickens had been broken and bloodied by their fall. Several had shards of glass protruding from their flanks. She did not see X–Fifty–Nine, but that did not mean he was not nearby. Such a dramatic manipulation as the chicken army should have been a ridiculous drain of his energy. Perhaps something as simple as materialization was beyond him now.

Azrael placed his hand under his coat, and held Theresa's mouth closed. He pulled her free, and placed her on his shoulder. Relieved, she slipped her tail into his ear, and attempted to synchronize with him for the third time. He did not reciprocate. Instead, he sent her a message:

Access the MTA's dispatch computer, and tell me when the last local train left Twenty–Third Street in Queens.

Not until you tell me what's going on.

Do you want to live, or argue?

No dice.

Azrael did not respond.

Are you insane? Please tell me what's going on here. Are you damaged, or something? Why didn't you manipulate the Tapestry? And even doing something as stupid as trying to shoot him — with your reflexes, how could you miss?

He stood silently, his eyes masked behind his glasses.

Azrael!

Theresa wondered if chickens could see in the dark, or for that matter, if they had exceptional hearing. Would they go for her eyes again? Puffing her neck in irritation, she hacked into the dispatch computer.

Goddamn you, it departed two minutes and thirty seconds ago.

Thank you.

Now tell me —

Azrael yanked her tail out of his ear, and tilted his head. His lips twitched as he spoke through calculations. He crawled forward, and touched the Manhattan–bound track with his shattered hand. He cocked his head again, and his lips counted silently from sixteen to zero.

"Over here!" he shouted.

The army stopped. They paused, as if considering their options. They turned in a single, synchronized motion. Some caught their claws on the tracks, and stumbled. Azrael breathed in sharply through his teeth as they floundered. Theresa guessed he had not anticipated the delay.

"Come on, you lice–infested bastards," he said. "What are you waiting for?"

His voice echoed down the tunnel. The sound was overwhelmed by another: the thunder of an approaching train. Azrael jumped back into the grime–coated alcove as it rattled by. "Goddamn MTA," he said, "first time in a century that it's not late."

When the track was clear, the chickens marched forward. As each row came to the third rail, they cleared it with a fluttering hop.

Theresa nuzzled Azrael's face. He looked down and smiled. She did not smile back.

He brandished the mangled umbrella and tore at its fabric, stripping it until he held an aluminum tree. He snapped off the wooden handle, and waited until the last chicken was on the track.

"Keep your head down," he said. He flung the umbrella spine sideways, twisting his wrist. It spun onto the tracks, simultaneously touching the farthest wheel rail and the electrified third.

Six hundred and twenty–five volts of electricity shot through the aluminum with an explosion of white fire. The surge of lightning grabbed the chickens along the grounded rail, and held them fast. They cooked and bubbled where they stood, filling the tunnel with the stench of charred meat.

Within seconds, the thin umbrella frame melted to slag, breaking the connection. Less than half of the fowl had been electrocuted. Those that remained once again began their approach, peering at Azrael and Theresa with beady eyes in the smoke–filled darkness. They were badly burned, with useless, charred limbs dangling from their sides. Azrael unwrapped his coat.

"Run," he said, "I'll hold them off."

Theresa winked. "Don't move," she said.

Azrael opened his mouth to protest, but closed it at the sound of clattering wheels. A train tore along the rails, grinding the remaining chickens into its tracks. Theresa feared it would stop, but it continued as if nothing had happened. Azrael stroked her neck. She shrugged.

"You asked me about the local," she said with no small amount of satisfaction. "That was the express." She flicked her tongue. "Not bad, even if I'm not a Dragon. Can you walk?"

"I've turned off my pain receptors," Azrael said. "Still, it will be difficult. How far is it to the nearest service corridor?"

Theresa reconnected to the dispatch computer, and examined its maps. "About a tenth of a mile," she said. She crawled onto his shoulder. "Now will you tell me why you can't manipulate?" she asked. Azrael remained silent. "I'll leave."

"Not in a dark, filthy tunnel full of rats, you won't," he said. "First we need to get to that maintenance door."

Azrael clomped through the tunnel, his torn boots occasionally sticking in the muck. His right foot was twisted, and his left leg dragged behind him. His uneven gait jarred Theresa's neck.

"I can help you heal," she said. Azrael did not reply. His breath came in drawn-out heaves, rattling deep in his chest.

They reached the service room. Theresa slipped her tail into the padlock, and manipulated its tumblers. It popped open, sprinkling rust onto her back. The darkness inside was absolute.

Once they were inside, Azrael collapsed to the concrete floor. "Repairing," he said. "I need forty-eight hours for minimum restoration."

"Good for you," Theresa said. "What am I supposed to do in the meantime?" But her partner was silent. She slipped her tail into his ear. He had put himself into an emergency coma without her assistance. "I would have helped you," she said. She unbuttoned his shirt with her teeth, snuggled against his warmth, and fell asleep to the labored rhythm of his breath.

She awoke to the sensation of something crawling on her. She sniffed it, and searched her database. It was a waterbug. She sucked it up. It was a mixture of salty and sour, with a crunchy texture. She nosed around, and found six more. She had not realized how hungry she was. She ate the roaches, wishing for water to wash them down. A leg caught in her throat, and she gagged.

"Dragons can go weeks without water, I'll bet," she muttered.

"Yes," a voice rumbled in the blackness, "they can."

A light flared, and she squeezed her eyes shut. When she opened them again, she saw X–Fifty–Nine sitting cross–legged on the cement. A ball of violet flame swirled above his face, casting his gaunt features into sharp relief.

"Theresa," he said, his voice thick and syrupy. He cupped his hands. There was water inside. "Come, little one, drink."

Theresa stared at his calloused palms, and at the reflections of the light that danced on the clear water. She had not been aware of how strong her thirst was. Now it constricted her throat. "No," she said.

X–Fifty–Nine chuckled. "Very well," he said. He pointed to a spot on the cement in front of her. "When this room was constructed, an air pocket lay deep in the ground. Before the cement dried, the earth settled a few inches, and a bowl formed right there." As Theresa watched, a depression, about three inches deep, dimpled in the floor. "There is a pipe above you, carrying clean, potable water. The fitter had an argument with his wife the morning he installed it, in which she mocked his sexual inadequacies. As a result, he did not pay attention to his work, and now that pipe occasionally drips." Drops of water splashed into the depression, filling it. "Is that more of what you're used to?"

Theresa stared at her reflection in the water. "And turning a subway full of people into chickens, and a pistol into an umbrella," she said. "I would love to hear the history of those."

"Ah, you see, that's the difference," said X–Fifty–Nine. "Your ex–partner was bound by the laws of cause and effect. I, however, can manipulate the Tapestry directly. Of course, it takes up much more energy, but a bit of theatrics now and then is necessary, don't you think? How else are we to become the stuff of their legends, the seeds of their nightmares?"

The color of Theresa's skin deepened. "What do you mean, 'ex–partner?'"

X–Fifty–Nine gestured to Azrael. "Access his memory, array Victor, nine thousand twenty–five, Mike, seventy–six."

"I can't —" Theresa said, but before she could finish, X–Fifty–Nine and his fire were gone.

Theresa crept forward in the blackness until her toenail touched the water. She opened her mouth to taste it, but pulled back.

She crept onto Azrael's shoulder. It was not impossible for her to break through his safeguards and access his memory, but it was extremely uncouth. Then again, so was hiding things from her, things she deserved to know. She looked up at him, swore, and rammed her tail into his ear.

Azrael's memory looked to her like a maze of glass boxes submerged underwater, netted together by glowing snakes. Every few seconds, a serpent wormed its way from one box to another, filling it with light. She searched along the array of cubes until she found the one of which X–Fifty–Nine had spoken. She took a deep breath, and dunked her head under the surface.

She became Azrael.

She saw through his eyes as he genuflected before a creature of light. Every hair stood on end. She felt a hardness between his legs pushing against the fabric of his pants. His teeth rattled. The Azrael in the memory averted his eyes. As hard as she tried, all Theresa could see of the being before him were its toes. They were white, immaculate, and shone as if the flesh under the skin was the sun.

"Azrael," a voice said, and it was a voice like honey. It made Theresa want to laugh, cry, dance, and shriek at the same time. If that voice had instructed her to slit her own throat,

Theresa would have done so joyfully. "We find it very hard to believe that you are questioning Us. You have never questioned before. What causes you to do so now?"

"But I have been faithful," Azrael said, and Theresa had never heard that emotion in his voice before, such dejected sadness. It felt as if his stomach was made of stone. "I did everything that You asked of me."

"And We thank you," the voice said. "But your time has passed. You have earned your rest."

"And now You're just throwing me away?"

"Must you use such words?" the voice asked, its delicious tones unwavering. "Other firms employ only the X models now; it is very important to Our stockholders that We do the same. In addition, Our customers do not want Us using an outmoded A. Z. unit for readjusting. Thank you for everything you have given Us, but it is time to move on. You will no longer be able to manipulate the Tapestry, Azrael. You will also remit your familiar to your successor for upgrading."

"But X–Fifty–Nine, he's... he's caused nothing but chaos, death, and unraveling for centuries."

Theresa felt warm, soft lips brush Azrael's penitent forehead. It was like being kissed by sunlight, by music, by joy. "We do not choose to recall that," the voice said. "Remit your familiar to him immediately. You have Our gratitude, Azrael, always."

"You can't do that to her!" Azrael cried as he raised his head. For a fleeting instant, Theresa glimpsed a face. It was flawless and featureless, a blank, shining oval. Then the brilliant light inside of the seraph bore into Azrael's eyes like blades of fire, and he screamed.

Darkness swallowed the world. Theresa felt Azrael's body fall limp. She expected him to sob, but he did not. The agony in his skull had faded, but she felt an equal suffering inside his chest. It was as if maggots were squirming within his heart. He silently held his genuflection, his body immobile.

Theresa could bear no more. She lifted her head from the water of her partner's memories, and disengaged her tail from his ear. She looked up at his comatose body, wondering if he was even aware of her intrusion. She slipped her tail underneath his mirrored glasses, and gasped. His eye sockets were two empty holes, scarred and blistered.

"Oh Azrael," she said, "I'm so sorry."

She kissed his cheek, and crawled down the length of his sleeping body. She felt around the floor until she found the pool of water. She lapped at it. It was cool, and sweet.

"All right," she said, "I know you're watching."

X–Fifty–Nine unfolded his body out of the air. His sphere of purple flames shone down on them once more. "I guess I'm yours now," Theresa said. "I have no choice."

"There is always a choice," X–Fifty–Nine said, extending his spider–like body to the ceiling. "But what will you do? You cannot help him. You can stay trapped in this world with him, fending for yourselves like beggars. A broken, blind man and his pet chameleon, lost in the tunnels with the other derelicts. Or, you can do as They want, and join me — as a Dragon."

Theresa puffed her neck. "I have conditions," she said. X–Fifty–Nine raised an eyebrow. "First of all, you take care of Azrael, make sure he leaves the Tapestry immediately."

"That is easy."

"Second," Theresa said, "you must undo what you have done. All those innocents you murdered today, for a start."

X–Fifty–Nine smiled. "What a heart you have," he said. "I promise, I will never have done those things. I am… respectable now."

"And I'll be a Dragon?" Theresa asked. X–Fifty–Nine nodded. "All right," she said, "let's link up." She climbed upon his shoulder, and extended her tail towards his ear.

She froze.

Her body jerked and trembled as indigo rings of light exploded up her spine, and into her brain. The scales of her tail bubbled and cracked, melting into a gleaming armor of cobalt steel. Her legs grew, and bulged with muscles. The change made its way to her stomach. Burning hooks slashed away inside of her, rearranging her organs. She retched and choked.

"I could simply upgrade you," X–Fifty–Nine said, "but it's much easier this way: if you were always a Dragon, if you were always mine."

Theresa shrieked Azrael's name. Her memories melted into globs of wax that ran down the inside of her skull to thrash and reform at the bottom. She twisted and screamed as her life was devoured by chaos.

"Are you all right?" X–Fifty–Nine asked.

Terrance took a deep breath. "Ugh," he said. It was hard for him to think. "It was that final attack, threw me for a loop. Give me a minute, would you?"

"Of course," said X–Fifty–Nine. He stroked Terrance's back. It sent a small shiver up the Dragon's spine. He licked X–Fifty–Nine's fingertips. He adored the salty taste of his master's skin. "It's a tragedy, Azrael going rogue like that," X–Fifty–nine said. "I always held him in the highest regard."

"He was a nutcase," Terrance said. "He turned a whole train of commuters into chickens just to get to you, remember?"

"To us, brother," said X–Fifty–Nine.

They gazed at the sleeping form at their feet. Terrance watched his glowing reflection in Azrael's mirrored glasses. He felt disorientated for a moment, as if almost remembering something from a forgotten dream. He shook it off. "He's just an obsolete A. Z. model," he said. "I can turn the bastard's brain off like a light bulb, if you want."

"No need," said X–Fifty–Nine. He clamped his giant hand on Azrael's jaw, opened his mouth, and placed it under the leaking pipe. Terence smirked as the drops plopped against the former manipulator's tongue. "He won't feel anything," X–Fifty–Nine said. "He'll drown long before his coma is finished, just another derelict that met his death in the tunnels."

"Couldn't happen to a nicer guy," said Terrance. X–Fifty–Nine raised an eyebrow, but said nothing. Terrance felt his scales grow warm. Had he said something wrong? All he wanted to do was be more like his master. Being hard was part of the job; it was all part of being a Dragon.

"Let's get out of here," he said. And with a ripple of the Tapestry, his master complied.

HEAVEN 2.0

Not one hour after her yellow Labrador Wynette had passed away, Gretchen Healy heard a knock on her door. It was soft and hollow, as if the knuckles themselves were made of wood. *Go away,* she thought. Her heart felt thick and heavy, as if someone had filled its chambers with lead. The last thing she wanted was to talk to anyone.

The knock came again.

She let out a long sigh from the pit of her stomach. Wynette had been her best friend. She had not judged, she had not been needy, and unlike people, she had always been there when Gretchen had needed companionship. All Gretchen wanted at the moment was to curl up in bed against the soft comfort of her quilt, and shut the rest of the world outside.

The hollow–sounding knuckles rapped the door a third time.

Gretchen wiped her puffy eyes with the back of her hand. She decided she would open the door, and tell whoever it was to go the hell away. She rose from the couch, walked to the door, and turned the handle.

"Good afternoon, Miss Healy," said the Asian man on her doorstep. He was short, thin, and carried the faint aroma of tuna. The Coke bottle lenses of his gold wire spectacles magnified his eyes into hazel saucers. His skin, the color of milk, hung from his skull in folds. His charcoal suit, by contrast, was silken, sharp, and impeccable, as if it had just come off the rack at Snobster Bros. "May I come in?"

By the time Gretchen had parted her lips to say no, the shriveled man had sidestepped her, and was inside her home. He removed his fedora to reveal not quite white hair that was thin and nicotine–stained. "I'm so sorry for your loss," he said, his head bowed.

Gretchen's eyes widened. "How did you know?" she asked.

"It is our business to know," the man said. He extended his left hand. Between the prune–like fingers was a business card. Gretchen took it.

"Hisao Oshiro," she read aloud, "Eternal Solutions." She turned it over. "Providing paradise for your beloved companions. Defeating Aquinas for over two hundred years." Comprehension dawned. "I see," she said. "Well, I've already made arrangements.

I'm having Wynette cremated, and I'm burying her under her favorite tree. So if you don't mind…" She gestured at the door.

"You misunderstand me," Oshiro said, raising his wizened hands. "I am not talking about repose for dear Wynette's body, I'm talking about a resting place for her eternal soul."

Gretchen's face flushed. "Ok," she said, "who sent you? Was it Lorraine in marketing? Because this is sick."

"I sent myself, Miss Healy," Oshiro said. "I come where I am needed."

"I don't need you."

Oshiro cocked his head, looking like a Siamese cat fashioned from crumpled plastic wrap. "Wynette does," he said.

Gretchen did not reply. Her comfort zone consisted of her job, her saxophone, a good book before bed, and, in the lonely dead of night, a glass or two of Merlot. She had been tossed without warning into the icy waters beyond that zone, and it took her a few seconds to proceed. "I thought all dogs went to heaven," she heard herself say.

Oshiro snorted, and chuckled to himself. "Miss Healy," he said, "without your intervention, poor Wynette could languish in limbo for all eternity. Doesn't she deserve better?"

Gretchen rubbed her temples. She felt a lump in her throat, and swallowed. "I don't believe this," she said. "So, what does an eternity in doggie paradise go for these days?"

"One year."

Gretchen blinked. "Excuse me?"

"One year off of the end of your life," Oshiro said. A pink tongue darted out of his mouth to lick his cracked lips. "Is that too much to ask?"

Gretchen shrugged. "Why not?" she said. "I hereby trade you one year off the end of my life for an eternity in paradise for Wynette. Now, will you please get the hell out?"

"Certainly," Oshiro said, his rheumy eyes glinting. He extended his hand. Gretchen shook it. It was cold and rubbery. "There is one minor matter, just legal red tape, to be honest."

"Whatever it is," said Gretchen, "I have complete faith in you to handle it." Hisao Oshiro grinned, and pumped her hand one more time. He placed his hat on his head, and left.

The next day, Gretchen held a small memorial ceremony in her back yard, herself being the sole mourner. She cleaned out a coconut shell, placed Wynette's ashes inside, and sealed it with cement made from flour, water, and eggs. She buried this biodegradable urn beneath a willow that Wynette had marked many times as her own. Being an atheist she said no prayers, but instead played Sinatra's "That's Life" on her smartphone. The ceremony completed, she went inside.

She heard a hollow knock.

Gretchen closed her eyes for a long moment. She crossed the house to her front door, and answered it.

Someone had tucked a black, square, cardboard envelope into the frame of the screen. She recognized it instantly for what it was: a disk holder. It had a rough but soft texture that reminded her of velvet. Inside was a charcoal–blue DVD–ROM, labeled *Heaven 2.0* in gold script. She looked up and down the street. She saw no one, just a calico cat lazing on the neighbor's lawn.

She loaded the disk into her laptop. The screen flickered, then it went black.

Pachelbel's "Magnificat" blurted from her speakers in eight–bit MIDI tones. A blocky VGA cartoon of a yellow Labrador appeared. It smiled, lolling a pink tongue from its mouth. The words *Heaven 2.0* flashed underneath in large Lucinda Console letters, along with "Press Enter to continue." The cartoon Wynette barked a digitized "arf."

A menu opened, offering a list of locations. There was a beach, a porch, a meadow, clouds with angels... All in all, she had twenty paradises to choose from. Gretchen streamed the program from her laptop to her smartphone, lay on her bed, and examined her choices.

She chose a playground, as she and Wynette had spent so much time walking together in the park. "Hunting, or canned food?" Wynette liked to chase birds, so Gretchen chose hunting. "Sleep, Y/N?" She chose Y. What would heaven be without sleep? The options went on and on, and before Gretchen knew it, an hour had passed. She knew this was a silly game, but giving Wynette the best afterlife possible, even if it was pretend, gave her a strange sense of closure. After eighty minutes, she had answered every question. The program compiled the results.

Her smartphone displayed a drawing of a playground. The cartoon Wynette bounded back and forth across the screen in front of a swing set. She nudged a swing with her nose. It swung back, and bopped her in the face. Startled, she yelped.

"Aww," Gretchen said. The icon changed into an open hand. She placed her fingertip over Wynette's back, and rubbed. The hand petted Wynette in slow, gentle strokes. The cartoon Lab smiled, her eyes closed. *Ok,* Gretchen decided, *that's enough for tonight.* She ended the stream, shut her laptop, and went to sleep.

The next morning Gretchen woke, took a shower, brushed her teeth, and went to work. She had an uneventful day filing medical claims, after which she went out for drinks with a few friends, came home, played her saxophone, and went to bed. This pattern repeated itself over the next few days, with a few variations. Soon it was Saturday, and she decided to listen to a CD while she relaxed and read. She ejected the disk drive of her laptop, and saw *Heaven 2.0* still in the caddy. She pushed it back in, and ran the program.

Weeds, leaves, and garbage overran the playground. Blocky brown pyramids adorned the grass, some with black pixels buzzing around them. Sleet ran across the screen in white diagonal lines. Wynette lay shivering under the merry–go–round. Her pixelated skin clung to her ribs. She pressed her matted, filthy fur into the mud. The speakers repeated a tone that started high pitched, and then fell. Gretchen's heart sank as she realized it was a digitized whine.

She opened the menu. What could she do? She clicked on the store, and breezed through the user agreement. For the price of two more months, she could buy a doghouse, one with a heated floor. She did. Playground maintenance would only shorten her life by one week per year. She agreed to that too, thinking it was quite reasonable. Fresh water was available for another week per year, or a once–only unlimited offer of seven months. "Meaty Afterlife Chow to supplement possibly scarce wildlife? A steal at only one year." What the hell, she decided, and bought the works, including chew toys, teeth cleaning, and de–worming. Her total bill wound up costing seven years off her life. She paused for a moment before agreeing. Then she laughed at her own silliness, and checked out.

When Gretchen was done, Wynette was cozy and warm, lapping at her fresh water, and savoring her Meaty Afterlife Chow. Gretchen draped a warm towel (at a cost of only one day) over her late Lab, and pet her until her hand hurt. Wynette no longer whined. She lay in her heated doghouse, her sides heaving in contentment.

Another week passed. At first, Gretchen spent half an hour a night in her late pet's interactive paradise, but by Wednesday, her dedication had been reduced to a few quick pets, and a toss of the ball. By Sunday, though Gretchen still felt a stabbing ache in her heart, Wynette's digital repose was all but forgotten.

That is, until there was another knock on her door.

Hisao Oshiro awaited her on her front step. The noon sun was hot and high, and brought every detail of his perfect suit and leather attaché case into sharp relief. His fedora cast a shadow over his sagging, milky face that was pitch black.

"Ah, Miss Healy," he purred from the back of his throat. "May I come in?" It was not a question, and Gretchen stepped aside without even realizing. He walked past her into the living room, sat on her couch, and put his attaché case on her coffee table. He thumbed the latches aside, snapping them up with simultaneous clicks. He raised his veined eyes up to meet hers, his expression a frown compounded by a mountain range of wrinkles.

"I'm afraid that legal issue I mentioned has come up," Oshiro said. He removed a manila folder four inches thick from the briefcase, and passed it to her. "This," he said before she could ask, "is your complete medical history."

Gretchen raised her eyebrows. "My what?" she asked. She unwound the binding string of the folder, and opened it.

The first document was a mimeograph, its letters fat, purple, and blurry, bearing the letterhead of her childhood pediatrician. It was a note to her mother, stating that Gretchen had a high fever, but because she was only five months old, the doctor would not prescribe antibiotics. She thumbed through the ream of paper, her heart pounding. Here were her middle school dental x–rays (never a cavity), there were the details of a visit to her college gynecologist for a yeast infection. Oshiro had collected thirty–six years' worth of personal details of her life, every blood test, and every prescription. The last stack of pages was a dot matrix printout of all the medical issues she had ever searched for online, from anxiety attacks to birth control. She squeezed the printout, her knuckles turning white. "Where," she managed to ask, "where did you get all this?"

"Our researchers are quite thorough," said Oshiro. He coughed. "Could I have a glass of milk, please?"

Gretchen mashed the printout in her fists. She threw the wad of paper in his face. "Get out," she said, trembling. Hisao Oshiro just looked up at her, expressionless. "Fine," she said, "I'm calling the police." She yanked her smartphone out of her pocket, and pressed the number nine. Her fingertip touched the number one, and froze.

She felt as if every vein, every capillary, every drop of liquid in her body — even her saliva and tears — had frozen. Illusory razors of ice slashed her skin, gutting her all the way down to her bones. Her jaw locked, smashing her teeth together. She shook, every muscle going into spasms.

And then the pain was gone.

Gretchen lay on the floor, convulsing and gasping for breath. She looked up through tear–filled eyes. Hisao Oshiro stood above her, his rubbery face still expressionless.

"I just repossessed one year from your life," he purred, his voice almost kind. "It took a day, I'm afraid, but you needed a demonstration."

Gretchen said nothing. Oshiro extended a hand to her. She slapped it away, and forced herself to her knees. Black spots exploded in front of her eyes. She crawled to her couch, and forced her aching body up onto it.

"Who — who are you?" she stammered.

"You entered into a contract, Miss Healy," Oshiro said, ignoring the question. His skin was rosier than it had been before, his ancient eyes clearer. "You then requested a greater loan, agreeing to a thorough background check."

"I never did."

He raised an eyebrow. "Did you not agree to the terms and conditions of the store?"

Gretchen's mind spun, the gears in her skull grinding against each other. "The user agreement was five pages long, and encrypted with legalese," she said. "No one ever reads those."

"The background check showed that you have a five percent chance of having ovarian cancer by the age of sixty, a ten percent chance of having arthritis by the age of seventy, a perchance towards depression, an alcoholic great uncle — it runs in the family, you know — a susceptibility for respiratory infections that could possibly lead to emphysema…" His voice trailed off. "Frankly, Miss Healy, the quality of the remaining years we've purchased from you is suspect, and we feel you've broken the good faith of our contract."

Gretchen stared at him. "I'm healthy," she said. "Those possibilities are all typical for anyone."

Oshiro tsked. "It is now noon," he said. "You have thirty–six hours to choose. Either we repossess Wynette's soul, or the remaining six years you owe us, plus a ten–year early payment penalty. The choice is yours." He picked up his briefcase, and walked past her.

"Wait," Gretchen said. She heard the door open and close. Hisao Oshiro was gone.

She slumped on her couch, panting and heaving, until she had the strength to pull herself to her feet. She staggered to the kitchen, and poured a cup of water. It was not until the cool liquid touched her lips that she realized how parched she was. She gulped it down, did the same to a second cup, and then a third. Once she had quenched her thirst, she booted up her laptop, and searched online for "Eternal Solutions."

The search came back with three pages of reviews, either on business rating sites, or various pet–themed blogs. They all sang Eternal Solutions's praises. None were specific about the company's actual practices, and Gretchen noticed similar patterns among them. Although the posters had different names, locations, and genders, the phrase "Finally gave me peace" was used in half of them. "I can sleep again" was another popular one, along with "I'd recommend them to anyone suffering a companion's loss." Gretchen groaned, running her hands through her hair.

She switched to forums to find discussions about the company. At first, she only found more of the same: a flood of glowing compliments. However, every forum had at least one comment that had been replaced with "Deleted by admin."

Gretchen searched through the directory of forum members. One was a contributor in every thread, but had no visible comments: Dogsbody12. She sent him a message: "Eternal Solutions harassing me. I need help."

The reply came back instantly: "Where are you?"

Gretchen glared at the screen. "Where are you?" she wrote back.

There was a pause. "Are you near any major city? New York, L.A., Chicago?"

"I'm relatively near New York."

"Is Maplewood, NJ a long drive for you?"

She hesitated. Maplewood was a hell of a lot closer than Manhattan. "I can manage," she typed.

There was a fifteen–minute delay. She wondered if her co–conspirator had left. "Meet Hounddog69 at the preservation dog park in two hours. Blue scarf. Good luck."

"Blue scarf? It's spring."

There was no answer.

The drive to Maplewood took twenty–five minutes. Gretchen parked near the dog park, and lay back in the front seat, rubbing her eyes. She still had five minutes to meet Hounddog69, whoever that distinguished gentleman was. She shouldered her purse, slid her hand inside, and touched the cool metal of her pepper spray can. Keeping her fingertips on it, she exited the car.

The park was nearly empty. She saw two men with a Yorkie, smoking cigarettes and laughing. Neither wore a blue scarf. A slender woman with black hair and a five–year–old boy took turns tossing a ball to a Dachshund so fat that its legs barely touched the ground. None of them had scarves. Gretchen tried to ignore the ball of anxiety that was forming in her stomach. The preservation was huge — was there more than one dog park in it? Her eyes darted from bench to bench.

On the furthest one sat a slender girl of about thirteen. She had an aristocratic face, framed by long, blond hair tied back in a ponytail. At her feet was an albino Boxer with a blue silk scarf around its neck. Gretchen approached. The girl met her gaze with a look of annoyance.

"You're two minutes late," she said. Gretchen opened her mouth. "Never mind," the girl said, "sit down." Gretchen did as she was told. "Pet Hound–dog Sixty–Nine."

Gretchen looked at the Boxer. It lay on its side, poking its nose into the grass, its eyes lazy and content. "Will he bite?"

"She," said the girl. "Can't you see the nipples?" Gretchen frowned. The dog was clearly a bitch. "And no, she won't bite. Boxers are naturally sweet. They have to be trained to be psychos. People who do that should have their livers ripped out."

Gretchen looked at the dog again. "You named her Hound–dog Sixty–Nine?" she asked.

"Just pet her, would you?"

Again, Gretchen did as she was told. "Don't stop," the girl said, staring off into the trees.

"Scratch behind her right ear, by the scarf."
Gretchen's fingers found the spot, and felt
something small and hard wrapped in the silk.
"Take it," said the girl, "but don't be too
obvious."

"Are we being watched?"

The girl shot her a look that would have
curdled milk. Gretchen did not know whether
to like the brat, or to slap her. She tried her best
to pretend that she was rubbing the albino
Boxer behind the ears as she maneuvered the
object out from underneath the scarf. It was a
USB drive. She slipped it into her purse.

The girl stood. "Come on," she said, tugging
on the leash. Hound–dog Sixty–Nine seemed to
roll her eyes as she got to her paws.

"Wait," Gretchen said. "What do I do with
this?" She reached out, and touched the girl's
arm. The girl whirled away, her eyes wide.

"Don't touch me," she said. She whipped a
pair of pink–framed sunglasses out of her
shorts pocket, and slid them over her face.
Gretchen stared at the girl as she walked away.
Then her stomach dropped.

"Oshiro!" she called after her, remembering
the icy torture of years being torn away. "Did
he, I mean…" Her voice trailed off. Neither the
girl nor the Boxer stopped.

Gretchen sped home, her fatigue forgotten. She ran upstairs and turned on her laptop, pacing as it booted. She snapped the USB drive into its slot.

The screen went black. Gretchen waited. After a minute, the low–resolution cartoon of Wynette appeared. She opened her pixelated mouth.

"Hello?" a voice said from the laptop's speakers. It sounded like a gruff old man from Brooklyn. The mouth opened and closed. "Hello? Anybody there?"

"Um, hello," Gretchen said.

"Oh, it's you," the voice said, "the one with the sax. How are you, kid?"

Gretchen swallowed. "Wynette?" she asked.

"Yeah, I was a dame with you, wasn't I?" Wynette said. "I hate being a girl, no offense, it just stinks having to wear diapers when you're in heat."

"I had you spayed."

"Oh yeah? Well once upon a time they couldn't do those fancy things."

Gretchen chuckled. Then she slumped forward, sobbing. It was as if a glass rod had supported her the last few days, and it had shattered.

"Hey, hey," Wynette said. The cartoon dog fell silent for a minute. "You'll be ok. As long as you can pull yourself to your feet and stand up on your own, you'll be ok."

Gretchen looked up at her laptop with stinging eyes. "But what about you?" she asked.

The cartoon dog shrugged. "I led a fun life. I've been reincarnated more times than I can remember," she said. "That's the difference between us and them. Don't believe their press. They live long, but only live once."

"Who?"

"Who?" Wynette looked left and right, her eyes narrow, her cartoon ears flat against her head. "The were–cats," she whispered.

Gretchen bit the inside of her cheek. She took a tissue from a box on her desk, and blew her nose into it. "The were–cats," she repeated.

"Shh, not so loud."

Gretchen rubbed her temples with her thumb and forefinger. "So, Oshiro is a were–cat?"

"No, not exactly, I just like calling them that. Sit down, this may take a while."

"Hang on a minute," Gretchen said. She streamed the program over her wireless router to her smartphone again. She lay on the bed, cradling Wynette's pixelated image in her hands.

"This feels a little different," Wynette said.

"I Wi–Fied you over here," Gretchen said. "I can stream programs from my laptop, and run them through my phone."

"Right, whatever that means," Wynette said. "How much do you know about Japanese mythology?"

"Zilch."

"Righty–ho." The Lab's digital tongue hung out for a moment. "The correct term is Bakeneko. It's a cat–demon from Japan. Or more precisely, it's a demon that's escaped into this world, possessed a cat that lived in Japan, and can sometimes take on human form, hence my snappy nickname for them."

"Uh–huh," Gretchen said. "And you're a were–dog?"

"No, I'm one of the Cynocephali."

"What's that?"

"Oh boy," the cartoon dog said. "Have you heard of Saint Christopher?"

"I've heard of a Saint Christopher's medal."

"Oy. Just listen," Wynette said. "The Cynocephali, my kind, were a race of canine–headed people from Africa. The unofficial legend of Saint Christopher is that he was one of us, but Jesus healed him, and he became a man. Still with me?"

"Yes. Keep going."

"The thing is, that wasn't quite what happened. What really happened is that we were given an offer. Take on the bodies of full dogs, and if one of us wipes out a Bakeneko, he or she gets reincarnated as a human. Until then, we keep living the lives of dogs, over and over."

Gretchen stretched, arching her back. "So how did you end up here?" she asked.

"Because you're my owner, and you signed my soul over in a contract," Wynette said. Gretchen clamped her jaw tight, grinding her teeth. "It's all right, it's happened that way for centuries. Demons are masters of legal trickery, it gets their rocks off. That's how Oshiro got a claim to feast on your life as well. That's what they do. They eat lives. Capisce?"

"But computers haven't been around for centuries."

"No, but computer programs are an art form like any other. Bakenekos have trapped us in poems, books, statues, paintings... That cute golden mutt in those 1970s movies was one of us. Now the poor schmuck's forever trapped in celluloid. That's how it works. Some of us become kiddie films, some of us become ones and zeros. Those are the breaks."

Gretchen nodded. "So what do we do now?" she asked.

"We?" Wynette said. "We do nothing. Me? It's been a good two thousand years. I had to get caught eventually."

"I'll kill him."

Wynette barked out a guffaw.

"What," Gretchen said, "you don't think I can defend myself?"

Wynette panted for a few moments. "You've got moxie, kid, I'll give you that," she said. "But even if I thought you were a killer, remember, this is a demon we're talking about. If they were that easy to kill, don't you think I'd have earned my opposable digits by now? The only way to off one is through the bite of a Cynocephali, and I don't see you growing a dog's head any time soon."

Gretchen ran her fingertips around the edge of her smartphone. "Were your teeth poisonous, or something?" she asked.

"It was just a matter of getting some of our essence into theirs," Wynette said.

Gretchen rolled onto her back, and stared at the ceiling. Neither of them spoke for a few minutes.

"I think," said Gretchen, "I may have an idea."

Gretchen perched at the edge of her couch. Her slender legs trembled, despite her earlier claims of bravado. She forced her eyes away from the door, and took in the objects around the room: the wireless router, her television, the silver tray on the coffee table in front of her. On the wall, the clock ticked away the seconds down to midnight.

She heard a hollow rapping on the door.

"Miss Healy?" Oshiro's voice was muffled and mewling. "It's time. I can wait all night, but we both know you're going to let me in."

Gretchen stood. She walked across her living room carpet with slow, deliberate steps. She unlocked the door, but kept the chain latched. She opened it until the links were taut.

"Hello," she said.

"Hello, Miss Healy," Oshiro said. The few inches of doorway cast a rectangle of amber light on his eyes. He narrowed them, sniffing. "So many scents in the air tonight," he said. "Fresh earth, and..." His eyes widened. "Is that tuna?" he asked.

Gretchen nodded. "I know what you are," she said.

"Really?"

"You're some sort of cat monster. And you hate dogs."

Oshiro chuckled. "'Some sort of cat monster,'" he said. His voice was still soft and purring, but there was a sharp edge underneath, like a barely concealed blade. "Dear child, just who have you been talking to?"

His fist shot forward and punched the door, snapping the chain and sending a chunk of the frame into the bridge of Gretchen's nose. She cried out, clutching her face as she fell back on the floor.

Oshiro stepped inside. "Now," he said, "what was that I smelled?"

Gretchen scuttled back as Oshiro strode across the room. He smiled at the silver tray on the coffee table, and yanked the cover upward.

"Tuna," he said, marveling at the whole fish that lay before him. He inhaled a deep, long sniff. "Mmm, fresh. It smells delicious, with just the slightest tinge of cremated Cynocephali mashed into the gills." He swept the tray to the floor. "Honestly," he said, shaking his head. "Do you think no one has ever tried that?"

Gretchen glanced at the carpet. Oshiro was almost upon her, but he was not quite in the right spot. She needed him to stand between the router and the couch. She lunged to the side. He caressed the nape of her neck as she passed. A wave of ice water rippled through her veins, and she crumpled to the floor.

"Sad," he said. "That was just a week, mind you." He grinned. "You know us 'cat monsters,' we like to play with our food." Gretchen forced her shaking hand underneath the sofa cushion. She found what she was looking for, closed her hand around it, and pushed herself to her knees.

"Oh dear," Oshiro said. He touched her neck again and she fell, her veins full of ice water. She curled into a fetal position, cradling the object in her hands. "Now," he said, as if talking to a child, "what have you got there?"

Gretchen took a deep breath. She had copied *Heaven 2.0* onto her hard drive, and broken the DVD–ROM into shards. She clenched the largest one in her fist, and drove its jagged edge into Oshiro's stomach.

It snapped on his silk shirt without tearing it.

Oshiro's eyes grew wide. "Clever bitch," he said. He hissed, his eyes blazing. He dove down, and clasped her face in his rubbery hands. His nails were hard, sharp claws that raked her skin. She screamed as her capillaries froze, the saliva in her mouth turning to ice. "Decades then," he said, as he ripped the years from her in a torrent of frozen needles. His skin and clothes ran together into a calico mixture. His ears flattened and pushed back on his head, while his nose and mouth stretched forward into a muzzle. "Who have you been talking to?" he demanded, his voice winding into a screeching yowl.

Then, abruptly, the pain stopped.

Oshiro stared at Gretchen, his claw–like hands falling to his sides. She fell back and rolled on the floor, gasping for breath. He took a wobbling step forward on his hind legs, as if drunk, "Who have you…?" he asked. His eyes, now slits, rolled back in his feline skull.

He exploded into a ball of orange flame that reeked of rotten fish and curdled milk. The windows shattered, along with the television.

Gretchen raised her head. Where Oshiro had stood, a hemisphere had been charred away in the coffee table, carpet, and couch. She felt between the remains of the cushions for her smartphone. She came away with a lump of plastic that was blackened and warped. She tried to curse, but no longer had the strength. She collapsed to the floor, and fell into a deep sleep.

Gretchen woke.

She stared up at the ceiling and deduced that she still lay on the floor, although now it was daylight. A pillow had been tucked underneath her head. She tried to reach for it, but something constricted her arms. Someone had wrapped her in her bed quilt. She lifted her head and the world spun around her, causing her stomach to churn. She flopped back down.

"Hello?" she croaked.

The sound of heavy panting approached. Gretchen struggled against the blanket, her panic rising. "Who's there?" she asked.

Hound–dog Sixty–Nine appeared above her, the Boxer's tongue lolling over her face. She leaned down, and licked Gretchen's cheeks with quick, sloppy laps.

"Hey!" Gretchen said, and tried in vain to roll away. The dog's blond owner walked into the room and knelt beside her, her pink sunglasses up on her head.

"Easy girl," she said, scratching the Boxer behind her ears. She appraised Gretchen's face. "Your cuts and bruises will take time to heal, but the years he stole from you are back. You need a new door, by the way." She sat cross–legged on the floor, and shook Hound–dog Sixty–Nine's jowls. "I felt Babirye being born into the world again. She's human, at last, but I couldn't tell you where she is."

"Babirye?"

"Wynette's real name, the one her mother gave her thousands of years ago. I remember all my brothers and sisters."

Gretchen stared at her. "You were a Cynocephali?" she asked.

The girl furrowed her eyebrows. "You blew up Oshiro and got my respect," she said. "Don't ruin it with stupid questions."

"Watch your mouth, kid," Gretchen said. "How did you get here anyway? You're not old enough to drive."

"My feet reach the pedals," the girl said. She smiled. "So tell me, because I can't figure it out. How did you do it?"

The melted remains of her smartphone on the carpet caught Gretchen's eye. "Wi–Fi," she said. "I streamed Wynette back and forth between my phone and laptop, via my router."

The girl's smile broadened. "And the signal, all the ones and zeros that made up poor Babirye's captured soul, went right through his wormy Bakeneko brain."

"Yep," Gretchen said. "It came down to something Wynette had said."

"What?"

"That it would take the byte of a Cynocephali."

The girl groaned, and pulled her sunglasses down. "You seriously suck," she said, swatting Gretchen's shoulder.

"Thank you," Gretchen replied with a smirk.

The girl turned her attention back to her Boxer. "We could use your help," she said.

Gretchen raised her eyebrows. "We?" she asked.

The girl nodded. "My brothers and sisters are reborn into the world all the time. There are only a few of us, and still hundreds of Bakenekos left. Would you like to give a good home to a reincarnated Cynocephali puppy? Help us with our network? We need someone like you."

Gretchen took a deep breath, and erupted into coughs. Her body shuddered. The girl helped pull her into a sitting position, loosening the quilt around her. Gretchen hacked up a wad of phlegm, and grimaced.

"Give me a few days to think it over," she said.

"Sure," said the girl, "but something tells me you'll say yes." She looked towards the kitchen. "I'm going to make myself a sandwich. Do you want anything?"

"Not now," Gretchen said. "I don't think I could eat."

"Ok," she said, striding towards the kitchen, Hound–dog Sixty–Nine in tow.

Gretchen watched the girl and her Boxer walk away. Then she leaned on the couch, took a deep breath, and pulled herself to her feet.

FLAWED COPIES

To Elisabeth MacHale, Greenwich Village was an advertisement for one grand, Bohemian party. Every bar, restaurant, and store seemed to promise music, theater, and artistic fellowship, if only she had the money to attend. The asphalt of the streets, in contrast to this bonhomie, was hard and rough through the paper–thin soles of her sneakers. Her tendons felt like elastic on the verge of snapping. She squinted up at the sun through the traffic of hovering cars. She wanted nothing more than to be in her room at the Burgundy House, with the curtains closed and a pillow over her head. But Fran had summoned her, and she had no choice but to obey.

Because of Anne.

A puppy chained outside of a brick–faced cafe barked and yipped as she passed. She knelt to scratch the top of its shaggy head. The miniature poodle licked her calloused hand in return. "Sorry, girl," Elisabeth muttered, "nothing good there."

"He's a boy," a voice said from behind her. Elisabeth turned. The girl was in her teens, probably just a few years older than Anne, with flawless skin the color of honey. She was one of those new brands, one Elisabeth was not familiar with, possibly a Bechdel. She wore clothes Anne would never be caught dead in: black spandex pants that clung to her walking stick thighs, covered at the top by a self–illuminating eggshell sweater. She looked like the kind of person Anne would shout obscenities at. The thought made Elisabeth's stomach hurt. She swallowed.

"Excuse me," the maybe–Bechdel said. Her chocolate eyes darted up and down West Fourth Street. Elisabeth shuffled a few steps away from the dog as the young woman undid its chain from the post. She shot Elisabeth a look over her shoulder. "I'm sorry," she said, "I don't have any change."

The tightness in Elisabeth's stomach rose to her throat. She made a choking sound, and then turned away. What would be the point?

It was almost two–thirty. She did not have to be back at the Burgundy House until nine. Tuesday was one of her two days off from the pizzeria, what the Burgundy people called "gainful employment." Maybe, Elisabeth thought, if she never left the home, and her meals consisted of her daily free slice of cheese. Her other day off was Thursday, but she had to go to Group on Thursdays, so that did not count.

She entered Washington Square Park. She tried not to look at the Regressives that slept on the benches. Her jaw twitched every time she passed one. Their stench, like rotting meat, assaulted her sinuses. They were corpses that had not figured out how to die. *They keep clinging on,* she thought, *while Chloe killed herself. Where's the justice in that?*

She made her way to the chess tables. A tall woman in her sixties sat alone, her gray hair dyed back to the trademarked MacHale shade of red, her freckled features twisted into a frown. To Elisabeth, it was like looking into a mirror that foretold the future.

Elisabeth clenched her teeth as she approached. She wanted nothing more than to tackle Fran where she sat, to knock her to the ground, and grind the look of smug superiority off of her face and onto the cement.

"Come on, leave her alone. She's been through hell."

"I don't care, she's been walking around in a fog the last two weeks. I can't have that on my job. What if she falls off the deck?"

"It's probably her meds."

"She needs medication. No wonder her sister killed herself, living with a freak like that. I wonder if there's Weight Watchers in heaven."

"Heh — oh shit!"

Elisabeth would forever savor that moment, when one Tarnowski had glimpsed her over the other's shoulder, the pimply carpenter's eyes going wide as Elisabeth clutched the forewoman's thick, greasy hair in her fist, spun her around, and smashed her moon–like face into the nearest I–beam.

Stop it! She tore herself away from the delicious memory, her body electrified with adrenaline. *That's how you got here. Do you want to go to prison instead of Burgundy?*

Elisabeth thrust her hands into the pockets of her sweat jacket, and squeezed them into fists. Her jagged nails cut into her palms. She should have taken her medication, but it made her feel like she was wandering at the bottom of the ocean. She forced herself to take long, slow breaths until the pounding in her ribcage subsided. She saw Fran watching all of this, judging and damning her with a glance. Elisabeth closed her eyes for a long moment, opened them, and approached.

"Hello, Elisabeth," Fran said, extending a perfectly manicured hand. Elisabeth shook it. She held her grip firm as Fran's fist squeezed hers.

"Hello, Mother," Elisabeth said. "Where's your set?"

"Set?"

Elisabeth gestured to the checkered table before them. "How are we going to play?"

The corners of Fran's mouth turned down, as if cranked to her chin by wires and gears hidden inside her cheeks. "I didn't call you here to play games," she said. "I want to talk about Anne."

Elisabeth ground her teeth. She heard them scrape against each other. "How is she?" she asked.

"Much better," Fran said. "Her grades have improved. At least she's stopped hanging out with her dirt–bag friends."

"You mean you won't let them in your house," said Elisabeth. "I'm sure in the last six months her life has completely turned around. Let me guess, she goes to church on Sundays as well?"

"Whatever it takes," Fran said. "Would you rather she was on the streets?" She paused to let the jibe sink in. "You have no real income, no home, and nothing to offer her."

"Forgive me," Elisabeth said, "I was in the hospital. If I don't have an apartment anymore, it's because you terminated the lease."

"I co–signed for it," said Fran. "What was I supposed to do, pay your bills until you got out?"

"You could have," Elisabeth said, "for Chloe's sake."

Fran remained silent for a long moment, her face like a statue. "Don't push me," she said at last. "You're lucky I was able to have you committed instead of incarcerated."

"That's what I've always liked about you," Elisabeth said. "Every favor you do is out of love." She leaned back, and closed her eyes. She wanted to be far away, somewhere no one could find her. She felt her fists shaking in her worn sweat jacket pockets. She unclenched them, took a deep breath, and counted to ten. "What do you want?"

Her mother reached into her purse, and pulled out an envelope. She passed it to Elisabeth. Elisabeth opened it, and skimmed over the document inside.

"Relinquishment of custody?" she asked, the words catching in her throat.

Fran nodded. "When you applied for reproduction privileges, you pledged to uphold the standards of the MacHale brand," she said. "You failed to do that." She stared into Elisabeth's blue eyes with her own. "We can do this the easy way, or the hard way. I'm retired, but I still have a bit of influence. Sign this, and

I'll get your status back to employable — in L.A."

Elisabeth stared at the forms. She could not comprehend their words. The letters might as well have been hieroglyphics. She stuffed the papers back into the envelope, and jammed it into her jeans pocket. "L.A.," she said.

"The carpenter's rate there is very good. Not quite as good as here in New York, but a lot of women would kill for that right now."

Yes, Elisabeth thought, *screw-gunning sheetrock onto studs, then moving on to the next one, and the one after that.* Maybe, if she was lucky, there might be a truck to unload now and then to break the monotony. Never fitting in because she was a brand castaway, and no matter how fast she tried to move, there were always young Tarnowskis or Doogans who were faster, girls who were not yet crippled by sciatica, girls bred with the temperament to zip aluminum studs with pride, to care so much about whether the Yankees or the Jets or the Knicks won tonight, or which girlfriend they were going to bed with. Never moving forward, always fighting just to tread water. What a fulfilling dream. Elisabeth swallowed. "So you want me out of the picture completely?"

"My granddaughter is a MacHale," Fran said. "I have to make sure she doesn't wind up like Chloe."

"And that was my fault?"

Fran's chapped lips pursed, becoming a ring of earthworms. She flexed her claw–like fingers. "You and your sister are Regressives," she said. "It happens, sometimes. But that doesn't necessarily mean Anne is one. The Scrubbers they had when you conceived her were much more thorough than the ones in my day."

"Yes, that must be it."

Fran's eyes narrowed. "Am I morbidly obese, or suicidal?" she asked. "Have I been arrested for violence? I'm pure. You should be thankful." She seemed to grow in her chair, towering up to the trees. "I don't pull punches, and while your sister was under my roof, it worked. She had no right to let her body blow up that way; she had the MacHale name to uphold. You let your sister get fatter and fatter until she was so unhappy and sick that she killed herself. If your daughter stays with you, she'll probably do the same."

Elisabeth lunged across the table, a scream burning her throat. Everything around her seemed to speed up, turning the world into a blur of red and black. Something felt wrong with her left knuckles. They burned as if a nest of hornets had stung her. Someone tried to grab her shoulders, and she ran.

Her thin soles smacked against the pavement. She gasped for breath. *Uptown,* she thought, *I have to get uptown.* She tried to put her left hand in her pocket, but it was a ball of pain. She looked down at it, and felt sick. It was covered in blood, and it hurt like hell. She leaned against the side of a building, gasping. A fountain of black marble squatted in a plaza half a block away. She staggered to it, and rinsed her hand in its icy water.

"Hey," someone shouted. A woman in a black uniform ran towards her, a bright red and orange patch on her shoulder. She was tan and voluptuous, with black hair and hazel eyes: a stock Cabrini. "Get the hell out of there."

"Sorry," said Elisabeth. Her fist was clean, but it was swollen and jagged, as if her skin had been pulled taut over broken wood. She tried to unclench her fingers. They would not open. The sleeve of her sweat jacket clung to her arm with rust–colored clots. She pulled her wrist back into it and wrung it out, letting loose a stream of water that looked like weak fruit punch.

The Cabrini reached for her radio. "That's it," she said, "I'm calling the police."

Elisabeth ran.

After a few blocks, she looked back. The security guard was nowhere in sight. The Cabrini had probably just wanted her away from the offices, Elisabeth mused, so decent women would not have to look at her.

She checked her watch. It was five after three. Could she make it by three–thirty? She staggered to the uptown avenue. A bus descended just as she reached the corner. She stepped inside, and slumped onto the nearest seat.

"Hey," the driver called back, "forgetting something?"

Elisabeth bit the inside of her cheek. She rose to her feet, and made her way to the front. The driver had her exact features, if perhaps aged a few years: another MacHale. "Please, cousin," she said, "my hand hurts."

"Don't give me that cousin shit," said the driver. "Either pay, or get off."

Elisabeth twisted her body, leaning against the post running through the center of the bus with her left shoulder. She stretched around her back with her right hand until she reached her left pocket. She dug her wallet out with her thumb and forefinger. Holding it inside her mouth, she flopped it open, and dug out a Metro card. She jerked it into the slot, almost dropping it in the process. The machine sucked it in, then spat it out with a disdainful bleep.

"It's out of rides, ma'am," the driver said, each syllable an enunciated curse.

"Hang on," said Elisabeth, her voice muffled through the wallet between her teeth. She felt three coins in her right pocket. She needed eight more. She dropped them into the coin slot. They fell inside with a kerchunking noise. She could feel the eyes of her fellow commuters boring into her back as she reached around her body again.

"Oh, never mind," the driver said. "Forget it, just sit down." She pressed a button, and Elisabeth's change slid out of a slot on the side. The fellow MacHale scooped it up, and handed it to her. "Don't let me catch you on my bus again without a card, you hear me?"

"Yes ma'am," Elisabeth mumbled through her wallet. The imitation leather tasted bitter on her tongue. She folded it up, slid it into her right back pocket, and plopped down on the nearest seat.

Her cousin's features softened. Most MacHales held cushy, white–collar jobs. For one to be a bus driver — or a carpenter, for that matter — had to mean some sort of fall from grace. "You hurt, or something?" she asked. "Do you need to go to a hospital?"

Elisabeth looked at her left hand. It had blossomed to a dark shade of purple. She caressed it with the tips of her fingers. Forks of pain shot up her arm. "Uptown," she said.

The bus let her off at Saint Moira's Academy. It was a big change from P.S. 193, Elisabeth thought with a slight pang, another thing for Anne that she could never afford. It was three twenty–five. She watched from across the street as the students exited. Two security guards stood at the gate. Were they waiting for her? Surely Fran had made it clear, with however much money it took, that Elisabeth was not allowed on school grounds.

She saw her daughter.

Anne slung her backpack over her mint–green uniform, her trademarked MacHale sapphire eyes skulking. She slouched as she walked alone, the other girls clinging together in the tight cliques of their own brands.

Elisabeth pulled the hood of her sweat jacket tight over her fiery hair. She tried to look inconspicuous as she walked to the nearest pay phone. She slipped in two coins, and stabbed at the buttons. Across the street, Anne stopped, reached in her pocket, and took out her phone. "Please," Elisabeth whispered, "please." Anne held it to her ear, and Elisabeth heard a click.

"Mom?" asked Anne.

"How did you know it was me?"

"Who else would it be, calling from a pay phone?" Anne looked in her direction. "Oh God, Mom, you're so stupid. You're calling from across the street."

Elisabeth smiled, in spite of it all. The expression fell from her face as the wail of sirens approached. "Uh–oh," she said.

"Uh–oh?" Anne asked. "What did you do this time?"

"Get out of there," said Elisabeth. "Meet me at the C train on Ninety–Sixth Street, downtown platform. Hurry."

"Mom, I'm not supposed to —"

"Just hurry," Elisabeth said, cutting her daughter off. She hung up and trudged down the street, away from the sirens.

She stopped at an ATM. She had just over two hundred dollars left in her checking account. She withdrew it all, and stuffed the bills into her wallet. Her hand burned and throbbed. She was sure at least one bone was broken, but there was no way she could go to a hospital. She reached the subway station, bought a one trip card, and raced to the downtown platform.

Elisabeth spun, her mind racing. Where was Anne? Did the police get to her, or did she just decide not to come? What sort of poison had her grandmother been filling her mind with? She walked the length of the platform, searching the crowd of Aldreds, Smiths, and Nicholsons. Her stomach churned. She wanted to lean over the edge and be sick.

She wanted someone to take her home.

"Mom?"

Elisabeth faced her daughter. "Anne," she said. She stared at her, at her red hair, blue eyes, and pale skin with freckles in the exact same places as her own. Two holes dotted her right nostril and eyebrow. "Grandma made you take them out, I see."

"Yeah," Anne said, staring at her. "Mom, what happened to your hand?"

"I always told you," Elisabeth said. "I always said you're too beautiful to have your face pierced up like that."

"Yeah," said Anne, "but at least you understood that it's my face."

The C train coasted into the station on its magnetic cushion, its engines humming in harmony. Elisabeth looked over her shoulder. "Come for a ride with me," she said. Anne took a step back, her patent leather shoes skidding on the platform. "You don't have to get off with me, but please, I need to talk to you, and it's the only safe place we can do it."

"Stand clear of the closing doors, please," the nasal recording said over the decrepit loudspeaker.

Anne met her mother's gaze, and then stepped inside. Elisabeth hurried after her, pulling her shattered hand in between the closing doors at the last second. She cradled it against her chest, and sat down.

"What did you do to your hand?" Anne asked. "That comes first."

"I broke it," Elisabeth said, "on Grandma's face."

"Wow," said Anne. She swallowed. "That would explain the police."

"Did they see you?" Elisabeth asked.

"No, I slipped off campus just as they pulled in." She sat lengthwise on the bench, pulling her knees up to her chin. "Why did you hit her?"

"I don't know," Elisabeth said. "I can't control myself anymore."

"You just... hit her."

Elisabeth bit her lip. "She said that I was responsible for Aunt Chloe killing herself," she said.

Anne stared at the ruddy lump of her mother's fist. "Was that the same thing your boss said?" she asked.

Elisabeth nodded. "Oh Anne, I know this has been so hard for you."

"No, you don't." Anne raised her head to reveal black rivers of mascara running down her cheeks. Elisabeth reached out to wipe them, but her daughter turned away. She pulled her hand back.

"Do you have any idea what it's like?" Anne asked. "Aunt Chloe kills herself, you're off in jail and then in the nuthouse, and now I have to live with Grandma. I hate her." Her voice broke over the last few words.

Elisabeth swallowed. "I'm sorry," she said.

"I don't blame Aunt Chloe," Anne said. "If I was programmed by someone like Grandma, always telling me I disappointed her and was letting the brand name down, I'd kill myself too."

Elisabeth shook her head. "I don't think it's that simple," she said. "Your aunt had something wrong in her head. The same thing is wrong in Grandma's head and mine. The difference is, your grandmother and I lash out at the world. Your aunt wound up lashing in at herself."

"And I'm supposed to feel sorry for her?" Anne asked. "We'll never be pure MacHales, we're just flawed copies."

"Listen to me," Elisabeth said. "You are not a flawed copy of anyone. You are Anne, and I am so proud of you."

Anne shifted in her seat. "So you hit her," she said. "How badly?"

"I don't know, I kind of blacked out," Elisabeth said. "Pretty bad, maybe as bad as what I did to my boss."

"Good."

Elisabeth closed her eyes. "You don't mean that," she said. "Let things go. Too many times I was angry when the sun went down on me."

"Wouldn't that hurt?"

Elisabeth looked at her daughter, then snorted out a laugh. "God, I've missed you," she said. She put her hand on Anne's shoulder. She didn't respond, but she didn't move away either.

"Why did you meet her in the first place?" Anne asked.

Elisabeth explained about the custody form. Anne's face turned bright pink. "Don't I have any say in this?" she asked.

"Did you ever?" Elisabeth tried to give her daughter a smile, but could not manage any better than a twitch of her cheeks.

Anne closed her eyes. "You'll have to do it now, won't you?" she asked.

"If I stay here, I'll go to jail no matter what," said Elisabeth, "back to the hospital at the very least. But if I sign over custody, it would be in your best interest. Grandma can take care of you. She can put you in college, open doors so you can do what you want. What can I do for you?"

"You could have fought her," Anne said, "for me. You could have fought so I could at least have been allowed to visit you. But you just gave up."

"I know," said Elisabeth, "and I'm sorry. Maybe that's why I hit her, I don't know." The train slowed as they pulled into the Fiftieth Street Station. Elisabeth twisted so she could reach her jeans pocket, and pulled out the crumpled envelope. "Do you have a pen?" she asked. Anne took one from her book bag. Elisabeth scanned the forms, and scribbled her name at the bottom of each one with her right hand. Her signatures were gibberish. The train stopped at Forty–Second Street, then moved on. There was one more station to go.

"Do me a favor," Elisabeth said. "Go to a post office, and mail them to your Grandmother's — to your house. Don't let the police know we talked, it will just get you in trouble." She squeezed her daughter's shoulder. "I'm going to get a train to however far away I can afford." She stood as the subway coasted into Penn Station. "I'll call you when I'm somewhere safe, I promise."

She stepped out onto the platform. She forced herself not to look behind her, not to see her daughter one more time. She walked towards the sign that said "Trains," her shoulders slumped.

Elisabeth stopped. Two cops stood at the entrance of the station. She wondered if they were looking for her, but it seemed unlikely. There was enough shit going on in the city to keep a Regressive in her mid–thirties from becoming public enemy number one.

"Do you have enough money for two?"

Elisabeth turned. Anne stood behind her.

"Anne, no," she said, but her daughter shook her head.

"I don't want to be with Grandma the rest of my life," Anne said. "I don't want to be stuck here, all alone, under her thumb, and never see you again. I don't want to end up like Aunt Chloe."

"No!" Elisabeth almost shouted. One of the cops raised an eyebrow. Elisabeth inhaled as deeply as she could, forcing herself to calm down. "Honey, I have nothing. You want to end up like Chloe? No? Then use your head, and make the most of life that you can. Set yourself up so that when you're older, you can do whatever makes you happy."

"Aunt Chloe wasn't happy with us?"

Elisabeth sighed. "Your aunt just couldn't be happy, period," she said. "She felt hurt and alone all the time, no matter how much we loved her, and eventually she felt like that's the only way she would ever feel. It didn't have anything to do with us." She caressed her daughter's face. "You need to learn to be happy with yourself."

Anne darted her eyes around the platform, then hugged her mother, squeezing her. Her hot tears pressed against Elisabeth's face. "Please," Anne whispered in her ear. "How can I learn to be happy without you?"

Elisabeth closed her eyes for a long moment. She kissed her daughter's forehead. "Go on," she said, "you may not want to watch this."

Anne smiled. "Nah," she said. "Besides, it will be something to tell your granddaughters someday."

Elisabeth laughed, and kissed her again. She turned, and walked towards the two officers. "Excuse me," she said. "My name is Elisabeth MacHale, and I'd like to turn myself in."

The two policewomen looked at each other. "For what?" one of them asked.

"Assault, I guess," Elisabeth answered. "About an hour ago, in Washington Square Park." She pulled her swollen left hand out of her pocket. "Also, I need medical attention." She waited as one of the officers spoke into her radio. After a few moments, they grabbed her by the shoulders.

She did not hear a word they said, she merely looked into Anne's cerulean eyes. She managed a smile and a wink before the two officers spun her around, and led her out of the station. Whatever happened next, she knew that at least she would have a home in her daughter's heart. But, she realized, she always had.

SHATTERED POSSIBILITIES

The icy mud seeped into my uniform as I lay prone, my eyes scanning the glowing forest for any sign of the Saucers. I tried not to think about the mosquitos that had laid their eggs in the slop, or whatever passed for mosquitos on Tartaros. I signaled for the squad to move forward. I could see Sergeant Rossi out of the corner of my eye. The tendons bulged on the back of his ruddy neck, as if he was some sort of doll woven from rope. He low–crawled through the gunked–up leaves, his legs wiggling like a lanky pollywog. The urge to giggle jumped to my throat. It happens sometimes, the laughter swells up in me and wants to explode, but I can't let it.

God is watching.

I buried my face against my jacket, and burst out laughing. I could feel Rossi glaring back at me from below those thin lines he calls eyebrows. I don't care, because there's no way me chuckling with my mouth jammed against my muck–covered arm could be louder than the sound of a man belly crawling through this slop.

Or a woman.

He signaled for me to advance. His hand motions were violent jerks, his legs twitching in tandem. I crawled. I turned my head to the tall grass where Fox and Flowers made their approach. I imagined Flowers wiggling her beautiful ass in the mud. And Fox got to watch, the lucky bastard —

My head smacked against a tree. I held my hands to my throbbing skull, and cursed. I actually saw stars in front of my eyes. I reoriented myself and crept back on course, refusing to meet Rossi's damning stare.

We took turns passing each other through mud, past trees, and over grass that all shone with a faint, blue glow. Fox told me once that the light isn't from radioactivity; it's probably some sort of symbiotic insect bioluminescence. To me that's worse, crawling through glowing worm shit.

We met at the edge of a clearing. The four of us crouched behind an outcropping of rock. The sky was gray and featureless, except for swirling plumes of clouds on the horizon: a sign that the Dark would be upon us soon. I gave Flowers what I assumed was a reassuring smile, which she ignored.

A family of creatures loped across the clearing. There were five large ones the size of cars, followed by a small one that looked to be about a foot high. They moved like spiders, walking on legs woven from needles. I could see through them, as if they had been blown from blackened glass.

"Aww," Flowers said, "there's a baby."

Rossi spat into the grass. "That's what you think," he said.

Flowers pouted. It made her look regal. "They're clearly a family," she said.

"No," said Rossi, "they're not a family. People have families. They're Saucers. They're insects. How stupid are you?" He stared at her with narrow, bloodshot eyes until she looked down, abashed like a scolded child.

Fox took a hesitant breath. "Sergeant," he said, "I still don't think this is Tartaros. And if it is, those aren't Tartarians." His voice had a weary, sing–song tone to it, as if he had been over this point a thousand times before.

"Don't correct me," Rossi said, squeezing his rifle. "Those Saucers bombed me once, when I was riding in the back of an ambulance — in a goddamn ambulance. No decency at all. Blew up the engine. The steering column went right through the driver's chest."

"There's no way those things could use a bomb, much less manufacture one."

Rossi lowered his rifle. He leaned in close to Fox's face, his brown, twitching eyes reflected in the Corporal's glasses.

"I told you," he said, his voice low and deliberate, "to stop correcting me."

Fox met Rossi's maniacal stare, but I could see the sweat beading on his forehead. He shrank, as if deflating from a pinhole in his stomach.

"Sergeant," Flowers said, pointing.

The family of spiders had snuck up on us from the other side of the boulders. Rossi swung his rifle up, and primed it. "Goddamn Saucers," he whispered. I fumbled with my weapon, my arm tangling in the shoulder strap. I yanked at the clasp, but it wouldn't budge.

The largest of the creatures opened its mouth.

Its words were pain. They were sharp and jagged, like shards of glass. They melted the world around me into darkness, but it wasn't the Dark. It was nothing like the Dark.

I held a mirror.

In the reflection, I advanced with the rest of the Forty–Ninth across the Sadira Valley of Artemis. We marched double–time over the rocky sand, our rifles clutched in our hands. I knew what would happen next, because I've relived the moment over and over ever since I was eighteen.

I watched myself leap over a trench. A Colonial, just a boy, slashed his bayonet up at me. I twisted to the side. It missed my belly, but the tip of the blade grazed the right side of my jaw. I stumbled, hot blood running down my chin, and into the neckline of my uniform.

I looked back, and saw Robinson. In boot camp, he would always hesitate before clearing a trench. The drill sergeant would curse at him to just jump the motherfucking thing, but Robinson couldn't help it; something inside of him made him flinch. This time when he hesitated, the boy jabbed his bayonet up and gutted him, tearing him open, and his intestines fell out onto the boy's face. The kid roared with triumph in his bloodbath, and the me in the mirror took this all in amidst the smoke, explosions, and gunfire, and kept running.

My hands turned numb. I dropped the mirror and watched it tumble away, as if through water. It shattered into four pieces, and I felt myself shattering too, as if a hammer had smashed my skull in chorus with the glass. I saw myself reflected in each shard, but each me was different. I was —

The vision ended.

The four of us stared at each other. Flowers's eyes were wide, with tears welling in their corners. I touched her arm. She jerked away. Fox clenched his jaw, grinding his teeth. He removed his thick glasses with shaking hands and wiped them on his uniform, smearing blue phosphorescent mud all over them. He put them back on, cursed, and then wiped them again with his fingers.

I wondered what memories they had seen.

Rossi convulsed, as if yanked by a string anchored in his skull. His lips curled back in the snarl of a rabid dog. He jerked up his rifle, aimed it at the glass spider that had sung, and squeezed the trigger.

It clicked.

"Malfunction," the weapon sang in a mechanical voice. "Malfunction. Perform SPORTS."

The crystal spiders danced away. Rossi's fingers scrambled across his rifle as he attempted to clear it. "What is wrong with you?" he said, his voice a whistling shriek. "Get after them."

I looked up. The swirling clouds on the horizon had whipped themselves into a frenzy, forming landspouts. "Sergeant," I said, "the Dark is coming."

"Go!" he shouted. He yanked the clip out of his rifle, and rammed it back in. "Go, go, go!" He tore across the clearing, his boots sloshing through the mud.

We followed. Rossi gained distance on Flowers and me, though Fox stayed right at his heels. I tried to forget what I had remembered, what I had felt. Why had the spiders dredged that out of me — that feeling of being a stupid, useless grunt, only able to watch while his friend got slaughtered like a sheep?

Was that all I was?

As if turned off by a light switch, the indigo luminescence went black. Indifferent to my turmoil, the Dark was absolute. I froze. I heard boots stumbling next to me, and then a body pounded into mine. We tumbled to the grass.

"Get off of me," I said, kicking at the figure. My heart pounded so hard, I could feel it in my head.

"It's me," Flowers said. "Stop it, idiot, it's me."

It took my brain a second to understand. We lay tangled, panting.

"Fox?" I shouted, my breath coming in hard gasps. "Sergeant?"

"Forget it," Flowers said, clutching my arm. I froze, then hugged her back. "We have to get back to the forest, before it comes."

My skull was dank with fog, as if my thoughts were fighting their way through steel wool and cotton candy. "We'll never find our way."

"The ground is soft here, though it's not as bad as the mud," Flowers said. Her breath was hot against my cheek. "I bet we can feel our footsteps, and retrace them."

I felt lightheaded. "All right," I said, "let's do it."

"Keep touching me so we don't lose each other, ok?"

"Ok," I said. I couldn't remember Flowers ever talking to me. I didn't remember her ever saying more than a sentence at a time to anyone.

"Come on," she said.

We crawled through the grass. She was right; it wasn't hard to find our way. I imagined crawling upon one of those crystal things in the blackness. The thought made my stomach churn.

Golden flames illuminated the landscape, casting long shadows across the clearing. We still had five hundred yards to go before we reached the forest line.

"We'll never make it," I said.

"We have to," said Flowers. "You know that."

"He can still find us."

Flowers raised herself to one knee. "It," she said. "It's never gone into the forest before, but it will get us out here in the open for sure. Ready?" She didn't wait for an answer. "Run."

My body wanted to obey someone, so it obeyed her. We ran for the trees. The hue surrounding us brightened to the color of yellow roses. I could feel the heat of God beating down my back, like blistering sunlight. I imagined the agony of His flames licking me.

He would see me soon. He would see me, and devour me.

We reached the trees and kept running, our boots fighting for traction in the slop. We worked our way uphill, the ground becoming drier as we climbed.

My side burned with every breath. I raised my arms above my head to try to work out the stitch. We reached the summit, and kept going until we were in the lee of the hilltop. Flowers dropped to the soft earth, and pulled me down alongside her. I looked to the sky. Yellow tongues of flame licked the treetops as the great sphere circled the forest.

"Do you think Fox and the Sarge made it?" I asked.

Flowers shrugged. "Fox, I hope so," she said. "Fuck Rossi."

She collapsed against me. I could feel the wetness of her tears on my cheek as I held her with shaking arms. I found myself kissing her forehead. She looked up at me. For a moment, all I could think of was how much she looked like both Rossi and Fox. It was an odd thought, and it made me giggle.

"What's wrong?" she asked. She smirked. "Am I that ugly?"

"No," I said, swallowing my laughter. "You're beautiful."

She leaned in, and pressed her soft lips against mine. I kissed her back, and then broke away. "Flowers," I said, "this isn't —"

"Shut up," she said. She climbed on top of me, rubbing her slender body against mine. My fingers slid underneath her jacket, and caressed her back in slow, circular strokes. She looked down into my eyes, her face proud and stern, like a statue of a goddess. "I've seen you looking at me," she said, "I know you want this."

"Yeah, but —"

"Shut up," she said again. She leaned forward, her hair dangling in my face. We froze, as if we had been petrified into statues of lovers. Our eyes locked, neither of us wanting to move. Her skin glowed like honey in the approaching yellow light. The spell broke and we kissed again, our lips barely brushing each other. She lay against me, her cheek touching my scarred jaw. "You like this," she said as she rocked back and forth, her voice low. "I can feel how much you like it."

I wrapped my arms around her, buried my face in her soft hair, and kissed her neck. "Yeah," I said, "I like it."

She rolled her eyes. "Then stop whining, Jesus," she said. Her breath was quicker now. "Show me. Make a baby in me."

I looked up at her. "Wait," I said, "you want me to get you pregnant?"

Her hands slid down to my belt buckle. She began fumbling with it as if it were a tavern puzzle. "Don't stop," she said, "please."

I stared at her. "I — here?" I asked, shaking my head. "Jesus, Flowers, what are you thinking?"

She jerked away, yanking her jacket down. "You're an asshole, Artes," she said, her voice throaty and hoarse. She curled up in a ball, facing away from me.

"Flowers…"

"Just leave me alone."

I wrapped my arms around her, spooning her body against mine. She wept, her chest jerking. I kissed her damp cheek. She reached behind her head, put her palm flat against my face, and pressed it against hers.

Then the Dark ended, taking the fire of God with it.

We rose, silent. The world was blue again. We retraced our footsteps towards the clearing. Every once in a while our hands would brush against each other. We said nothing. I glimpsed her out of the corner of my eye. I had never noticed how sad she looked before. It was as if a spring inside of her was winding down, and would soon creak to a rusting halt.

"Stop that," Flowers said. "Don't look at me, I don't like being looked —" Her voice broke off.

The smallest of the crystal spiders squatted before us. It reared on its needle legs, its head lolling back and forth on its shoulders. I could see the forest through its body, distorted and refracted.

"The poor thing," Flowers said. "It's just a baby."

"That's no baby," I said. "Remember what happened at the clearing?"

Flowers ignored me. She took a few small steps and crouched, her right hand extended. "Hey, little guy," she said, "did you lose your mommy?"

"Flowers," I said. My chest squeezed my heart. I wanted to get far away before the thing assaulted me with another memory. "Please get back."

She shushed me. She held her hand out further, cooing and making baby talk at the thing. I wanted to run, but I couldn't leave her, and now it was too late. It slid back on its pins, and its razor–lined lips parted —

There was a crack of thunder.

The glass spider let out a wheeze, and dropped to the glowing earth. Red and grey muck splattered across the tree behind it. I turned. Rossi stood with Fox beside him, his smoking rifle still pointed at the fallen creature.

"Jesus," I said. "What the hell did you do?"

"Don't you start," said Rossi, his eyes twitching. "Those mindfuckers are in our heads. Making us... making us..." He focused on me. "And where the hell were you two?"

"Sergeant," Fox cut in.

"Shut up," Rossi said, swinging towards the corporal. "When we get back, I'm..." His jaw dropped. I followed his gaze, and swallowed.

Flowers had picked up the baby spider. Half of its head was gone, and something resembling strawberry porridge oozed out. She cradled it, smiling.

"Look," she said, stroking the transparent skull just below its unseeing eyes. "Look, Bethany's ok. Her head is fine."

I swallowed. "Flowers," I said. I didn't know what else to say.

"After she was born," she said, "they wouldn't even let me hold her." She cuddled the creature in her arms. "Oh, Bethany."

The Dark came without warning. There was no period of blackness this time, just the harsh illumination of yellow flames on the horizon. The voice of God echoed across the sky, His howling rage at the murder of one of his creatures shaking the trees. I took a step toward Flowers.

"We have to go," I said.

"No," she said, clutching the shattered body to her chest. "This is bonding time, it's important."

"To hell with this shit," Rossi said, and grabbed for the spider. Flowers spun away, tightening her arms around the corpse. I felt the burning eyes of God turning toward us. He could smell us now, I was sure of it. He could smell Flowers's motherhood, her love and suffering.

"Listen," I said, "we have to protect Bethany. Do you understand? If we don't go now, He will hurt her. We need to get her somewhere safe."

Flowers looked at me with flowing eyes. "Do you promise, Artes?"

"I promise," I said. "Come on." I reached out to her. She took my hand, and we ran.

Our boots sloshed through the forest as we dodged through the obstacle course of gnarled roots. I could feel His celestial flames at my back, the razors of His teeth gnashing at my hair.

We came to the mouth of a tunnel. It was about fifteen feet in diameter, winding deep into the earth. Nests of roots poked through the crumbling walls, intertwined like ancient, arthritic fingers.

Fox ran a hand along the clay wall. "Amazing," he said. "Whatever did this sheared right through the rock." He pointed. "It makes a swirling pattern, see? This is the first sign of technology I've found here." A black slug crawled onto his hand. He wiped it off on the moss.

"Great, just great," Rossi said. "Come on, get in deeper."

"What's the point?" Fox asked. "It's shining right through the rocks and the trees, even through the earth. Believe me, it sees us. But it sees more than our bodies, it sees who we are."

Rossi exhaled between clenched teeth. "What bullshit are you talking now?"

Fox chuckled, resting his head against the clay. "Yes, all I talk is bullshit," he said, "because that's all I am." He spread his arms apart. "Don't you get it? We're just shadows. We're not real."

I touched Flowers's arm. "I'm real," I said.

"Yeah?" Fox asked. "Then what's your first name?"

I looked at him, unable to answer.

"Face it," he said, "whatever happened to us has destroyed our minds, or maybe you just always were thick, I don't remember." He tapped his forehead. "It's a form of amnesia. Our implicit and procedural memories are fine, but most of our current and long–term ones are gone." He pointed at us, one by one. "How about eating, because I don't remember eating since we've been here. I know what sleeping is, but I can't tell you the last time I did it."

He pointed at the creature lying dead in Flowers's arms. "That thing, somehow it picks out a memory that defines you. I know it did for me. For her, it was obviously losing her child. But I'll bet you she forgot all about it before today. How about you, Artes, what did it make you remember?" I swallowed, remaining silent. "Sergeant?"

"All right," Rossi said, "enough. You shut your mouth right now."

Fox spread his feet and locked his hands behind his back, his elbows jutting out at his sides. "Oh, yes, Sergeant," he said. "Whatever you say."

Rossi's breaths came in long, slow gasps. "Right now, we go deeper into this cave," he said. "We seek shelter. That's all we have to worry about. I don't want to hear anything else." He turned to face Flowers and me, my hand still holding onto her arm. "And goddamn it you two, act like soldiers. You're the most worthless pieces of shit I've ever seen." He turned and marched down the tunnel, smacking roots out of his way. We followed him in silence.

At the end of the tunnel was a metal cylinder. It was twisted and pitted, the plating marred by carbon and corrosion. Fox placed his hand on a jagged edge, and whistled.

"What is it?" Flowers asked.

No one answered, but I felt that I knew, it was right at the tip of my tongue. The object was a foot smaller than the diameter of the tunnel. I looked at the edges, glowing in the flickering amber light that grew brighter every second.

Rossi ran his hands over the surface. His face had a perplexed expression, as if chasing a memory. He tore away the moss and corrosion until his fingers sunk into a depression. He pulled on it. It didn't budge. He gritted his teeth, and yanked.

The metal gave. With a groan and a snowfall of rust, the side of the capsule swung open.

Inside was what looked like an upright bed, connected to a breathing mask that dangled from a ribbed hose. A viscous fluid had pooled on the padded floor. Fox jabbed the blob with his finger. It bounced away.

Rossi stared into the cabin. "So where's the occupant?" he asked.

"Look at all this rust and corrosion, at the roots in the tunnel," Fox said. "I'd say this has been here fifty, sixty years, at least. Maybe a hundred, or even two. I have no idea what the atmospheric norm for this planet is."

A button blinked on the console attached to the mask.

I pressed it.

A hologram flickered into life. It was of a young man, I'd guess nineteen years old. He was muscular, a grunt. His features were ordinary, save for a puckered scar woven across his jaw. I looked at him, and felt my eyes burn.

"This is PFC James Artes," he said. "The Saucers hit us hard, got the reactor. Captain Biesadeski gave the order to abandon ship. We were still in light–phase. I feel dizzy." The boy in the hologram giggled, but there was no humor in his eyes. "I — I don't know what this place is."

The image blurred, wavered, and overlapped with another. This time it was of a young woman. Flowers gasped. It looked like her, but it couldn't be her. The woman in the hologram had dark blond hair, and Flowers's was thin and white. I looked at my hands. They were wrinkled and spotted.

I had never noticed.

"They say to never eject while in light–phase," the simulacrum of Flowers said. "I'm amazed I survived, but something is very wrong here."

The image flickered again, transforming into a man in glasses. "This place is unreal," continued a younger hologram of Fox. "Is it possible I'm still in mid–phase? They say nothing could survive that, but it's never been tested."

The image changed once more, but I didn't recognize the figure. It looked like Sergeant Rossi, it had his name and rank, but his eyes and voice possessed a serene confidence that our squad leader's never could.

"I'm going to go look for survivors now," said the young sergeant. "These men and women are the best soldiers in the army, I'm sure they survi —"

The hologram flickered again. The console emitted a long beep, and then the flashing light fell dark.

We stood in silence. I reached out, and stroked Flowers's cheek with the back of my hand. She was still beautiful. It didn't matter if her skin was wrinkled, if time had etched lines around her mouth, or if her hair was white and thin. She stepped away, looking down at the creature in her arms. She walked to the capsule, and placed it down on the soft pad at the bottom. She took her jacket off, and swaddled the corpse in it.

A wave of exhaustion broke over me. I leaned against the corroded metal of the capsule. I rubbed my jaw, running my fingertips along the scar's puckered texture. "Fox," I said, "how long have we been here?"

Fox shook his head, his white hair falling over his glasses. "I have no idea," he said. "If we're in mid–phase, there's no way to tell. We could be outside of time altogether, or we could be trapped between milliseconds. How much time passes between instants? Who knows?" He began to babble, his words coming faster and faster.

"Light–phase weaves tunnels in–between the fabric of dimensions," he said. "Maybe we're just the shattered possibilities of what might have been, or who might have been. The facets of a life, torn from the different layers of the multiverse during a convergence of events." He slumped, his energy spent. "Whatever or whoever we are, we don't belong here. We're like an infection upon reality. We need to be cauterized, because like I told you, we're not real."

A wail filled the tunnel, a wretched, primordial shriek. It took a moment for me to realize that it came from Rossi. He shook, silhouetted by the approaching fire of God. His eyes were wide, his pupils constricted to pinpricks. He brandished his rifle high above his head and lunged, driving the butt into Fox's skull. The old man fell to the ground, his glasses shattered.

"Stop saying that," Rossi said. His voice was high, hoarse, and fast, like an auctioneer being strangled in mid pitch. "Stop saying that. You're always running your mouth. You think you know everything. Just shut the fuck up!" The last word was a guttural scream.

I grabbed Rossi's arm before he could swing again. We struggled, two ancient men wrestling like comical gladiators. He shoved me to the ground.

My coccyx snapped with a crack. Agony shot up my spine. I could barely breathe. Rossi staggered back, and raised his rifle. He stared down his sights at me, his finger twitching on the trigger.

Flowers dove in between us. She crouched, staring up at Rossi. He snorted, and shifted his aim towards her. I tried my damnedest to push her out of the way, but I couldn't. My body refused to move; the pain in my pelvis was too horrible.

The tunnel pitched back and forth, as if giants were smashing the earth with their fists. I looked down the tunnel, and stared into the mouth of God. He devoured the soil, the roots, and even the rocks in His path.

His voice was thunder, a baby's wail, metal tearing into metal, a symphony, a cacophony.

His face was a swirl of amber fire — yellow skin stretched taut over a ribbed skull, with rows upon rows of swirling razors inside of His maw. His breath was a hurricane. His uncountable obsidian eyes looked inside of me, and I felt His hunger. He wanted to devour me, to shred me into nothingness, and shit my atoms into the mud of His world. He was a sun, casting long, dark shadows onto the cave walls. I couldn't look at Him; I felt my brain being cooked through my eyes when I looked. But I couldn't turn away either.

Rossi froze. He did not turn to see what loomed behind him. His face was forever a mask of terror and panic, of jealousy, fear, and rage. I wondered what he had seen in his own mirrored visions, what he had remembered.

Then God was upon him.

His flaming razors minced and incinerated Rossi from behind, churning the sergeant's stomach to flames and ash, while that perpetual look of hatred remained on his face. Then that too was gone, sucked into the Sun.

I looked at God, and He looked into me. I felt Flowers clutching my arms, felt the warmth of her face against mine, but inside, I felt nothing.

And then He was upon us.

I woke.

An angel peered at me, his crystalline, triangular face the color of midnight. He waved his hands through the amber haze that surrounded us, like a maestro conducting a symphony. He had so many limbs that I could not count them. His knuckles were faceted like glass, his fingers spindly needles.

The smallest of his spider–like hands was shattered, and oozing with pink porridge.

I wanted to raise my head, but I could not move. I could not tell if anything held me, or if I was paralyzed. The black, shining eyes of God whirled above and around me, staring into my soul, and judging my worth. The angel tilted its head back and forth as if I were a new specimen it had discovered. It unclenched its fist, and the mouth inside sang —

A body lay before me on an operating table. It was a boy, not any older than sixteen, and his leg had been shredded by a Gatling gun, like so much chuck meat hanging from a bone. Six somber men held him while he drove his teeth down into a twisted towel. I wielded a bone saw. Guilt and sorrow welled up in my stomach like bile, so strong that I was going to burst, but I had to I had to —

I jerked out of the illusion. I was back in the world of yellow fire, with the angel watching over me.

I opened and closed my mouth. That had not been my own memory; it was something I had once read in a history book. "Where's Flowers?" I asked. "Is she ok?" The angel gazed at me again, its lidless eyes glistening with fascination. "Flowers!" I shouted.

Another mouth–hand opened.

I was seven, at my father's farm, skipping a stone across a stream. But it wasn't a stone, it was a die. It broke into four pieces when it hit the water, causing ripples in its wake, each ripple interfering with the pattern of the others until the reflections on the water became stars streaming by with the blue–shift of light–phase. The universe shattered like a jagged mirror into four pieces, each with its own die, and I shattered again with the mirror, except the reflections weren't mine, they were —

As if waking from a dream, I returned to the flaming room. I looked up at the angel. It nodded at me.

"I don't understand," I said. "Why won't you just talk to me?"

It gave me a weary, reproachful look, and then sang once more.

It was my turn to be on an operating table. A gaping wound marred my chest, seething with pus. I could smell the infection, like a chicken leg left out in the sun. A grandfather clock was at the far end of the theater, and a man in a blue–green gown stood in front of it with his back to me.

The hands of the clock inched forward from midnight. They crawled at first, then accelerated, the seconds becoming minutes, hours, days, and years, until the surgeon grabbed the hands, and halted them. He turned them backwards and swung the decades away, back to the beginning. Then the hands inched forward again. He turned to face me. His mouth was covered by a mask, and I couldn't see his eyes, because his glasses reflected the harsh lights above us. He walked out of my field of vision. He returned, holding an iron rod in a gauntleted fist, the end blazing red, yellow, and white. He cocked his head and I tried to open my mouth, but nothing would come out, and he lowered the fiery rod and touched it to my festering chest —

"Sergeant, over here."

Flowers stood above me. She was young and beautiful, her oval features tinged by blue light. My back was cold, and soaked with mud. Rossi came into view. He stared down at me with concern.

"Soldier, can you stand?" he asked. He reached down, and grabbed my hand. I let him help me to my feet, the muck dripping away. I looked at our hands. They were young and strong, our grips firm.

"Are there any other survivors?" Flowers asked.

"It's amazing the four of us landed so close together," Fox said. "By rights we should all be miles apart."

Rossi stared into my eyes. "Are you ok, soldier?" he asked. I didn't reply. His voice became hard. "Name, rank," he barked.

I blinked. There was something I wanted to say — something I needed to say — but I could not. All I could do was look at the three soldiers before me with features so similar they could have easily been brothers and a sister. My mouth wouldn't work. My brain was full of rusted gears that wouldn't mesh together. I looked down, and saw my name tag on my chest. I read it upside down. "Artes," I said at last. I looked down at the insignia on my arm. "Private First Class."

Flowers grinned at me. "Don't feel bad," she said. "We all had to do that."

"Shock from the landing, I expect, scrambled our memories somehow," Fox said. He looked up at the featureless sky, at the swirling cloud bank amassing on the horizon. "I can't for the life of me figure out where we are. But this isn't Tartaros."

"Bullshit, where else could we be?" Rossi asked.

"It's insanely dangerous to jettison in light–phase," Fox said. "We could be anywhere, in any time. We could even be outside of time all together."

Rossi raised an eyebrow at him. He took a deep breath, and forced a smile. "I'm sure you'll figure it out, then," he said at last. He patted me on the shoulder. "Come on soldier, cheer up," he said. "Look at it this way: If anything here is dangerous, at least it can only kill us once."

SOUL MATES

Melvin Jacobs hated parties. More so, he hated being dragged through them like a chubby dog on a leash. To be fair to himself, he had lost quite a few pounds recently, but at two hundred and sixty, he still stretched his double–breasted jacket's seams. Tonight his personal hell was a fundraiser for the Pleasant Hills Community Theater production of *Guys and Dolls*. Denise was their costume designer, and Melvin just had to come. Because he was her husband, her —

"Jessica!" Denise shrieked, yanking Melvin towards a gaggle of socialites. The center of attention was a woman who wore the perfect amount of jewelry to enhance her perfect makeup which accented a dress that showed — in Melvin's opinion — the perfect amount of cleavage. He caught an expression of weary dread on the woman's aristocratic face, one she smoothed over with a smile that was... perfect.

"Denise," Jessica said, a noble greeting a serf. "I'm glad you could come." Jessica Sage–

Huber, director of the board of education, mayoral candidate, and wife of the owner of the *Hills Reader,* had been cast in the lead role of Sarah Brown. "Why Melvin, you've lost weight," she said, jabbing a manicured finger at his belly.

"Just a few pounds," Denise said before Melvin could inhale. "He's got a way to go, and absolutely no willpower. But I'll make sure he does it." She gave Jessica a conspiratorial wink. "He's my soul mate."

"I'm sure he is," Jessica said. "Well, your contribution to the sets —"

"Costumes," Denise interrupted, "I designed your dress."

"Of course," Jessica said. "Just like in school, you were always so talented." This earned titters from her entourage. "Either way, you're one of the unsung heroes. Here, try one of my cupcakes. I mean you, of course, Denise. Melvin is on a diet."

Melvin's stomach twisted. His wife seemed to have put on every pound he had lost, and she took it as a personal insult. Denise stared at the pastries, and swallowed. "No," she said, "I couldn't."

"But I slaved over them," said Jessica. "Surely you don't have to worry about one cupcake." She pouted. "You wouldn't want to hurt my feelings, would you?"

Denise grimaced, picked up a cupcake, and took a bite.

Melvin grabbed the corner of the table. It was happening again, the feeling that something was sucking away at the inside of his body. It had started a few weeks ago, now it happened daily. He just hoped there was nothing wrong with his plumbing.

Jessica nodded with satisfaction as Denise swallowed the last crumb. "It's very good," Denise said. "Excuse me, I have to go to the bathroom."

"Of course you do," Jessica said. Melvin watched her as his wife exited. He didn't get the joke until one of the harpies stuck a finger in her mouth, and pretended to retch. So that was it. He tried to feel bad for Denise, but could not. He thought he should feel something.

Now he did: a warm swelling in the center of his waist. He felt satiated, just a bit heavier. He frowned. It was as if something had just materialized inside of him. Denise stepped out of the bathroom, her face blanched. "Are you all right?" he asked.

"I want to go home," she said. "And you can stop drooling over her, you pig."

"But what about the party?" he asked.

Her lower lip quivered. "Melvin," she said, "I'm telling you, we're going home."

On Monday, at the Heart Band factory, Melvin could barely concentrate. His stomach had started its games at eight o'clock that morning. It had felt empty, then full a few minutes later. The cycle had repeated itself for hours, but each expansion just slightly outweighed each loss. He examined his sausage–like fingers. Was it his imagination, or were they plumper?

"Jacobs, are you listening to me? This is a lawsuit we're talking about here. That Sage–Huber bitch wants to make us her scapegoat."

Melvin looked at his father–in–law. Mister Heart ("Familiarity in the workplace breeds anarchy" was his creed), was thin as a walking stick, and stood barely five and a half feet tall. He masticated his thick, silver moustache before continuing.

"Miserable children's safety do–gooders," the old man said. "There have always been rubber bands in classrooms, and by God there always will be. This is just a publicity stunt for her goddamned campaign."

"Yes, sir," Melvin said. He shifted uncomfortably in his chair. Something was definitely wrong with his stomach.

"Jessica and Denise went to school together. Hell, they're both involved in that ridiculous theater. And now, just because one kindergartener brat gets snapped in the eye, she's suing us for millions." Mister Heart threw the brief across his desk. "She always was spoiled. I remember after their senior year, old man Sage sent her on a six–month skiing trip to Aspen. I had to do the same for Denise the following winter just to shut her whining mouth. So, what recourses do we have?"

Melvin had long ago realized that his job description included free legal consultation. "Well, sir," he began. Without warning, his stomach constricted, as if squeezed by an invisible hand. He checked his watch. It was eleven forty–five, Denise's lunchtime. The swelling followed on cue, hard and fast. "Shit," he muttered, clutching his side.

"Exactly," Mister Heart said. "Smear job. Let's dig up all the filth on her we can. Good job, Jacobs." He peered at Melvin. "Are you losing weight?"

Melvin swallowed. "Something like that, sir."

"Mmm," said his father–in–law. He seemed about to say something more, then changed his mind. "Start digging."

"Honey, there's something I have to ask you."

It had taken Melvin the entire drive home to come up with that line. He glanced at his wife across the dining room table, but she just picked at her steak. "Denise?"

"I heard you," she said.

Melvin took a deep breath. "Denise, have you been… purging?" he asked.

He finally had her attention. She bit her lower lip. "Of course not," she said.

"I heard you in the bathroom at the fundraiser," Melvin lied.

Denise's face crumpled like a wax flower left out in the sun. "You don't understand," she said. "You're a man. Who cares if you're a slob? You don't know how it feels."

"It's dangerous," he said. "You have to stop."

"Make me."

He stared at her, incredulous. "You could die."

She pushed her plate away. "You can't tell me what to do," she said.

Melvin rubbed his forehead. He cut himself another slice. "Your father asked about you today," he said.

She blanched. "And what did you tell him?"

"I told him you were fine," he said. "Of course, if he knew you were bulimic…" He let the word dangle in the air.

Denise's pupils constricted to pinpricks. "You wouldn't dare," she said.

Melvin took a bite. "Denise," he said, "if you do it just one more time, I'll know. Trust me. And when I know, he'll know."

She put her head in her hands. "I'm disgusting," she wailed, "and the play is less than two months away. I overheard Jessica say that I'd never even fit into one of my own dresses."

"You're fine."

"No, I'm not. I don't want to be a three hundred pound sow like my mother. And here you are, practically emaciated."

"I lost twenty pounds in three months," Melvin said.

"So? What will everyone think if you weigh less than I do?"

So that was it. He forced a loving smile. "Come on, eat something," he said. He put a piece of steak on his fork, and held it out to her. "Just take one bite, please?"

She did, and the subsequent tugging within his belly felt delightful. "Oh Melvin," she said. "Thank God Daddy saved you when your practice failed. I know you'll always take care of me. You're my soul mate."

"Yes," he said, spearing another slice. "Have some more. You'll feel better."

Two days later, Melvin drove to a house that was, like most of those belonging to Heart

Band's employees, on the poorer side of town. The neighborhood had been erected during the great depression, right next to Hills Lake. Melvin could not go a week without overhearing complaints about all that great property going to waste.

He turned his car onto the gravel driveway, ignoring the swelling in his waistline. It felt as if tiny balloons were inflating inside of his cellulite. His weight loss had slowed, plateaued, and was now creeping back up again.

An unshaven man stood on the lawn, drenching brown grass with a garden hose. He turned it off when Melvin got out of the car. "Mister Jacobs," he said, "is something wrong? Today's my day off."

Melvin extended his hand. "Relax, Davies," he said. "I'd just like to talk to you."

"About what?"

"Jessica Sage–Huber."

Davies bit his lip. He looked down at his dead lawn. "I haven't seen her in years," he said. "I didn't know anything about that lawsuit. I just read about it in the paper."

Melvin patted his shoulder. "Why don't we talk inside?" he asked.

The ranch's interior was a labyrinth of magazines, DVDs, unwashed dishes, and junk mail. "I'm a bachelor," Davies said, "Jessica saw to that."

It took him half an hour to tell his story, a tale ripe with blame and victimization. They had been college lovers for a year, their passion expressed in every nook and cranny of Rutgers's campus. But when he proposed marriage, she had laughed in his face. She explained in no uncertain terms that while he was fun, she damn well intended to marry someone who could give her the lifestyle in which she had been raised. He then sunk into depression, lost his scholarship, and followed his father's footsteps onto the Heart Band factory floor.

Melvin nodded, a well–practiced expression of sympathy on his face. Mister Heart had authorized up to a grand for the real dirt, but the woman was truly clean. It had cost him a hundred dollars alone just to find out that she had dated Davies two decades ago. He felt exhausted. He felt bloated. He clenched his teeth together, silently cursing his wife. She was definitely up to something.

Davies finished his diatribe. "Yeah, she always had aspirations," he said. "Nice body too, best I ever had. Comes from being so athletic."

"I've heard she's a great skier," Melvin said as he stood.

Davies squinted at him. "What are you talking about?" he asked. "I took her to

Mountain Creek, once. She couldn't ski to save her life. She'd never done it before."

A mental tumbler clicked into place. "Thanks," Melvin said, handing the machinist a fifty–dollar bill.

Davies took it with a shrug. "Huh," he said. "I don't mean to sound greedy, but is that all my story is worth?"

"That depends on how this pans out."

Melvin sat at his kitchen table, fuming. Jessica Sage–Huber had not been to Aspen that fateful post–high school year. Just finding that out had cost him another week, and two hundred dollars. Discovering where she *had* been would cost even more. Worse, the bribes and his waistline were growing in tandem.

Denise strode into the kitchen, a sewing pattern under her arm. She opened the refrigerator, took out a celery stick, and began crunching. She was definitely on the diet train, and it was an express.

"Melvin, have you been putting on weight?" she asked. He raised his eyes to meet hers, careful to keep them expressionless. Her grin radiated triumph. But she did not know — she could not know — about their special relationship. Otherwise, she would be force–feeding him bacon covered with chocolate frosting.

"A little, I guess," he said, "not like you."

"Thank you, dear. It's willpower. It's self–control. I must have learned it from Daddy."

Melvin clenched his teeth, thankful for the barbs. They helped squash what little guilt he still felt. "What's your secret?" he asked. He frowned at the apprehensive look on her face. "You haven't gone back to throwing up, have you?"

"No," she said. "Daddy said not to tell you, just to surprise you with the results. But I'm doing so well." Her face lit up. "I joined a gym."

"Really?" he asked, wide–eyed. He was impressed.

Her voice faltered. "He said some cruel things, but they did the trick." She glared at Melvin. "And he's right. I know how you men think. Well don't worry, I'm not going to disgust you anymore." Tears glistened in her eyes.

"Honey," Melvin said. He stood, and hugged her. "You never disgust me." He felt that all too familiar restriction in his armpits, the one that meant he needed a larger shirt size. "Hey, what gym did you join? I'll come down and support you."

"Really?" she sniffed.

He kissed her cheek. "Really."

It took another week, another three hundred and fifty in bribes, and another notch on his belt before Melvin could siege the office of Jessica Sage–Huber. Even then, she kept him waiting in the lobby for an hour and forty–five minutes. When he was finally admitted, she did not bother to get out of her leather chair, or even look up from her monitor. "What did you want to see me about?" she asked.

"It's about your campaign," Melvin said, placing his briefcase on her desk. "Do you intend to go through with this lawsuit?"

"First of all," she said, "the lawsuit has nothing to do with my mayoral campaign. It's for the children's safety. I'm sorry that's not one of your father–in–law's concerns."

"It would bankrupt our factory," Melvin said. "Many workers in the town you propose to run would become unemployed. They'd have to leave, and find somewhere less expensive to live." She said nothing. "Now, I know that you wouldn't want that to happen. Although, in theory, I suppose many real estate companies would, lakeside property value being what it is, and all."

"I told you," Jessica said, "all I care about is children's safety." She paused, the corners of her lips twitching. "That is a funny theory you have, but think about it. I'm a Democrat. Do you think your blue–collar workers would vote against me?" She nodded towards the door. "Now, get out of here."

"Certainly," Melvin said. He snapped his fingers. "Oh, there is just one more thing." He opened his briefcase, took out three eight by ten inch pictures, and laid them on top of her keyboard.

Jessica's left hand clenched the side of her desk. One photo was of a muscular Hispanic man, about fifty years old. The second was of a man in his mid–twenties. The third was a copy of a birth certificate. The birthplace it documented was in New Mexico, and the mother's name was Jessica Sage.

"This is Esteban Rios," Melvin said, gesturing to the picture of the younger man, "your son." He paused to let the words sink in. "Your husband does know, doesn't he? I mean, otherwise it will be a shock when every paper in the county but his carries these pictures."

Jessica slumped back in her chair, staring at the photographs in silence. "I was just eighteen," she said at last. "My parents wanted me to get an abortion, but I couldn't do it. He was our gardener."

"Abejundio? Yes, he's quite handsome. Do you know that your father stopped sending him money when your boy was eight?" Melvin placed a photo of a family on top of the others. Their faces had dignity, but their clothes were threadbare. "This is your son, his father, his grandmother, and two cousins, posing in front of their trailer in Albuquerque. That's where they all live together. And here you are with all of this." He gestured at the oak–paneled walls. "Still, at least they kept him safe from rubber bands."

Jessica picked up the picture of Esteban, her lips trembling. She held it to her chest, and closed her eyes. "So I just have to drop the lawsuit, is that it?" she asked, her voice cracking.

"Well," Melvin said, "there are two more things I'll need personally. The first, I promise you'll like. But the second…"

Melvin whistled as he strolled into his office. Two weeks had passed since his meeting with Jessica Sage–Huber, and in that time his waist had slimmed from forty inches to thirty–eight. He stopped short when he saw Mister Heart sitting at his desk. "Good morning, sir," he said.

"Good morning, Jacobs. Shut the door."

Melvin did as he was instructed. His father–in–law handed him a faded, sepia–toned portrait in an oval frame, one that Melvin had seen hanging behind the old man's desk. "Do you know who that is?" Mister Heart asked. He did not wait for an answer. "That is my great–great–grandfather, Joshua Heart. A proud, willful man, who was partners with another man of vision: Stephen Perry, the inventor of the rubber band." Mister Heart held his hand out, and Melvin dutifully handed the faded portrait back. His father–in–law gazed at it with reverence.

"In 1852, back in the days of industrial conquest, my ancestor journeyed to Asia to acquire a field of *ficus elastica:* The Indian Rubber Plant." He spoke the capital letters. "They can grow almost anywhere, under the right conditions. But old Joshua knew that men of prestige would pay top dollar for rubber bands made of true Indian rubber."

"Very good, sir," Melvin said dutifully.

"The fields were owned by a former monk. At his request, Joshua demonstrated the wonders of the invention," Mister Heart said. His chin jutted out as he stared off into the distance. "Can you imagine it? Those scrawny little savages had never seen anything so elegant. It stretched. It bound without knots. They stood in awe, as if Joshua were the almighty himself." He slammed his palm on Melvin's desk. "But when the ex–monk tried to stretch one, the rubber snapped."

"Oh no, sir."

"Yes!" Mister Heart shouted, wagging his finger. "But instead of a tragedy, it was a blessing. It turned out that the ex–monk had recently married, and the errant rubber band put out his mother–in–law's one good eye." The old man cackled at this. Melvin forced his cheeks upward into a proud smile.

"The holy man was so pleased that he gave Joshua a blessing. For you see, Joshua, for all of his laudable character, had only one minor flaw: his weight." Melvin's jaw involuntarily clenched, but he said nothing. Mister Heart nodded. "Yes, Joshua was heavy, with a nagging wench for a wife. So the monk passed on an ancient curse, binding them together. Their weights were balanced. If one gained, the other lost, and vice versa. Joshua fattened his wife up in no time at all, and slimmed down to a gentlemanly one hundred and eighty pounds. And the curse — or blessing — was passed on from generation to generation, taking effect on the thousandth day of marriage."

Mister Heart opened Melvin's drawer, and pulled out a newspaper. It was last Sunday's *Hills Reader.* He flung it at Melvin. "How did you figure it out?"

Melvin did not move. *The Sunday Hills Reader* had printed an insert about the modern obesity epidemic. It featured a close–up of Denise Jacobs straining the seams of her purple spandex as she jiggled on a stationary bike. The article praised all the people of Pleasant Hills who struggled with their weight, saying how wonderful it was that they never gave up. By Sunday evening, Denise had plopped her not–quite–aerobicized ass down in front of the television with a bucket of cookie dough. For all Melvin knew, she was still there. Yes, he thought, feeling that wonderful tug at his insides, she was.

"Figure out what, sir?" he asked.

"It was for her, you smug bastard!" his father–in–law shouted. His face was bright pink. "Your flabby ass was supposed to keep her slim and happy. Why do you think I let a worthless piece of shit like you marry her?" He reached under the desk, and pulled out a can of lard. He tore the cap off. "Now eat this," he said, shoving it in front of Melvin's nose. "I've seen you chow down before. Gobble it, gobble it all." Melvin just stared at him. Finally, the old man sank back.

"Fine," he said, his fury spent. "Then you're fired. Get out."

"No," Melvin said. His father–in–law's hollow cheeks turned a deep shade of violet. "Give me a break, Georgie–boy. What will you do, tell her? I wonder if my dear mother–in–law would like to know why she's spent her last forty–five years at three hundred pounds, or if Jessica Sage–Huber would like a star witness when she sues you for extortion." The old man's face darkened to a definite purple. "By the way, what's the big deal? I'll divorce her, and you can find some other fat schmuck."

His father–in–law scowled. "No," he said. "You're soul mates forever, not even in death do you part." He turned away, as if realizing what he had said.

When it came to suburban community theater, *Guys and Dolls* was well regarded among the safe staples. The same real estate agent who had starred in last year's production of *The Music Man* had been cast in the role of Nathan Detroit. The year before that, it was *Annie Get Your Gun* (Buffalo Bill played by the local neurosurgeon that was playing Sky Masterson), and before that, *The Sound of Music,* with Maria portrayed by the same actress who was starring this year as Sarah Brown, the ever–perfect Jessica Sage–Huber.

Denise had not wanted to come, of course. She had not left the house for a month. "But think of the costumes," Melvin insisted. "When people see Jessica twirling in that dress, it's you they'll think of. It might even get you some designing work." She sat beside him, crammed into a Lane Bryant pants suit. He, for the first time in eight years, wore pants with a waist size of thirty–six.

The curtain rose, and the musical began. The sets, the actors, the orchestra, and even the costumes — to Denise's credit — were beautiful. The only thing wrong was the star. It was nothing major, just a few cues missed here and there and a few cracked high notes, but something was definitely not right. Melvin had worried; Jessica had fought against this final extortion for an hour before giving in. But here she was, and it was obvious from her floundering that she was committed.

Finally, her solo came. Sister Sarah was in love, and for some reason, it made her feel like a bell. Denise had based Jessica's costume on a 1930s Salvation Army dress, but its hemline was lower, to provide more flounce when she twirled. Melvin squeezed the armrest of his chair in anticipation.

With tears in her eyes, Jessica fumbled a kick, and caught her heel in the bottom of her dress. *Now fall,* Melvin commanded silently, *your performance ruined by Denise Jacobs's one-piece blunder.* But instead of tripping her, the dress tore in half at the seam, revealing a body that was, for all intents and purposes, perfect.

The theater thundered with applause as the mayoral candidate wrapped the remains of the dress around her, and stumbled offstage. Melvin laughed so hard that he barely felt the small amount of weight filling his stomach. Denise was throwing up.

Melvin watched his wife out of the corner of his eye as he drove. She seemed so dejected, so ashamed. But every few minutes, her eyes would gleam, her cheek would twitch, and then she would swallow, as if fighting to regain control.

"I'm glad to see you're not taking it too badly," he ventured. At this, she burst into laughter.

"I got her," she shrieked. "I got that miserable, stuck–up whore back!"

Melvin glanced at her out of the corner of his eye. "What?" he asked.

"I snuck into her dressing room this morning, and I cut every other stitch of her seam," Denise said. Her laughs were high–pitched squeals of delight that made her jowls ripple. "I was afraid it would take a while to rip, but she did it herself. She stunk!"

This was bad, Melvin thought, very, very bad. Denise reached over, and squeezed his thigh. "Hey," he said.

"What?" she asked. "Since when are you such a prude?"

"Since never," Melvin said. He rubbed the nape of his neck. This was not going according to plan at all. She was supposed to cry all the way home, eat herself into a stupor, and sob herself to sleep in humiliation. But she hadn't been humiliated, damn her, she had been triumphant.

Melvin opened the garage door by remote as he pulled into the driveway. He parked the car, listening to it idle. It had a beautiful engine, damn near silent. He turned off the ignition. "Go on up," he said. "I want to check the oil."

"Sure," Denise said, winking. She put her finger on his lips. "Don't make me wait too long." Melvin managed a feeble smile as she exited the garage, pausing in the doorway to kick back her ample heel.

He sat in the driver's seat, dazed. *My God,* he thought, *can I do this?* He looked down at his waist, a waist that was just now approaching what he deemed presentable. Could he allow any chance of becoming that butterball again? No way, he decided, no way in Hell.

He pressed the garage door remote and turned the ignition key simultaneously. The clanking of the closing door drowned out the starter. He stepped inside the house, and listened. He could not hear the engine at all.

He had attempted to forge a suicide note, but he could not make it sound authentic. Perhaps it was just as well; his wife had put on such a show at the musical that people would believe anything. He ventured up the stairs, wondering how to convince her to go to sleep.

Denise roosted in the center of their bed, wearing a little red nothing that was three sizes too small. It cut pink lines into her shoulders. She held two glasses of champagne. She fluttered her eyelashes, and held out the one in her left hand.

"A toast," she said. "A toast to my dress."

Melvin managed a grimace. He took the proffered glass, and sipped. *What the hell is this cheap crap?* he wondered. It tasted awful. "You showed them, honey," he said.

"Oh, I'll show them even more," she agreed, sipping her own.

He felt lightheaded. Perhaps he should have eaten more — or she should have eaten less. He chuckled, and took another sip.

"No, really," she said, misunderstanding. "I'm getting gastric bypass surgery."

He spit his second mouthful of champagne across the room. "What?" he slurred. He stopped, frowning. Something was definitely wrong.

"Drink up, love," Denise said. Melvin lurched forward, nauseous. His inner ear decided that it did not like quick motions, and he stumbled against the wall. The glass fell from his hand, half empty, to the carpet.

"Don't be upset," his wife said. "After all, Daddy's paying for it." The room spun. "He insisted."

"You poisoned me?"

"That was Daddy's idea too." She took another sip. "After all, I can't have you losing weight on me. Then I'll be stuck at the blubbery end of the seesaw."

"Bitch," Melvin sputtered.

"Oh, come now," said Denise. "You're not going to die. One of Daddy's friends will do a little operation on your brain, and then you won't worry about anything at all. You'll have everything you need: an IV, a catheter, and a feeding tube." She finished her champagne. "Don't worry, I'll make sure you're fed very, very well."

Melvin lunged, forcing her down onto the mattress. His limbs stung as if they were asleep, but her obesity made it difficult for her to fight. He clamped a pillow over her face, and lay on top of it. She thrashed beneath him, but he managed to hold her down. After what seemed like an eternity, she stopped jerking, and lay still.

He rolled off of her and onto the floor, pulling the pillow with him. He choked and sputtered. It was impossible to breathe. Was it the poison, or the carbon monoxide? Did it matter? He staggered on his knees to the phone. His fingers felt like dangling worms, and could not press the buttons. At last, he managed to hit the 9–1–1 auto–dial with his nose.

An angel was on the line, singing hosannas unto the Lord. Melvin had something important to tell her, but it did not matter. He liked her singing. He wanted to ask her to sing some more, but all that came out was a choked gasp. Sleep, he marveled as the world around him spun into night. The angel was singing him to sleep.

Light.

A soft, white light bloomed in the haze. Melvin felt a spark of hope in his chest. Somehow, he had made it into heaven, imagine that. He sighed. *How can you sigh when you're dead?* he wondered. *Do souls fill their lungs from the aether?*

"Ah, you're awake."

Melvin tried to place the voice. It was familiar, and it was bad. Maybe he wasn't in heaven after all. It was hard to think.

"I'm happy, you know."

Melvin blinked. *Focus,* he commanded his eyes. They refused. Everything was a white, soupy blur. The air had a clean, antiseptic odor, with an underlying musty smell, like a hint of New England clam chowder.

A grey blur loomed down until it filled Melvin's frame of vision. It reluctantly took on detail: thick, silver hair, icy blue eyes, and a push–broom moustache. "You woke up just in time, you son of a bitch," it said.

"Georgie–boy," Melvin croaked. His mouth felt as if it was full of sand. "Where am I?"

"Of course, you ask about yourself. Not a worry for my Denise. She's dead, by the way."

Melvin swallowed. "Where?" he asked again.

His father–in–law coughed into a handkerchief. "You're in a hospital," he said, "you have been for five days. There was some debate as to whether you'd make it or not." He cracked his knuckles. "The police think that she poisoned you, turned on the car's ignition, then went back to lie down and die. It makes sense, right after her public humiliation."

A wave of relief crested over Melvin. He realized he must have smiled, because his father–in–law's jaw shook, his eyes narrowing to slits.

"You think you're one smart bastard, don't you?" he spat. "I wanted to be here, to stare at your smug, worthless, slender face." He regained his composure, and glanced at his Rolex. "I'm missing it, you know."

"Missing what?" Melvin slurred.

"Her funeral."

Melvin's grin shrank a few millimeters. "Why?" he asked.

"They're all wondering that too," Mister Heart said, checking his watch again. "My family. They think I'm here because I'm desperate to know what happened, waiting at your side 'till you can tell me why my baby died. Don't worry, I know."

It suddenly became hard for Melvin to breathe. "Am I supposed to feel bad?" he asked, wheezing. "You two were going to lobotomize me. Now she'll just lie in her grave, mysteriously getting fatter. You said it yourself. We're bound together, even... after... death..." It felt as if an elephant had just plopped down on his chest. He sputtered. His father–in–law did not pay attention; he merely looked at his watch.

Melvin choked out a gurgling scream. His cheeks burst, like dough popping from a biscuit canister. Lesions tore across his skin as two hundred and seventy–two pounds of cellulite erupted from his flesh. He tried to gasp, but his lungs refused to comply. The metal bed frame collapsed under his weight, crashing to the tiled floor with an echoing clang.

"I know," his father–in–law said. He leaned in as Melvin croaked out his final, strangled breath, and smiled. "That's why I just had her cremated."

THE AUTUMN PEOPLE

My mind wandered inside the grooves of an oak tabletop magnified through a shot of Jack Daniels. Worms had etched trails into it over the decades, entwining with a carved initial or two. I ran my fingers over the splintered edges, imagining what future archaeologists would read in these hieroglyphics. I hoped it would be something about a boy who loved a girl, or about a busboy who wished herpes upon his boss.

Anything but the two thousand souls I saw burn that morning.

"Goddamn it, Joe, you're doing it again."

I lifted my eyes to meet Samantha's shining gaze. My tongue was pinned between my molars. I must have chewed on it again, an old habit. "Sorry, Sam," I said, "I didn't realize."

"It doesn't bother me," she said with a shrug. She sipped her beer as though it were a chardonnay. "You know we'll be closed tomorrow, and we're three days behind on inventory as it is."

"Uh–huh," I said. They had looked like flies, little black dots against the blue patches of morning sky not yet obliterated by smoke, black dots that became little flailing stick figures as they fell. I tried closing my eyes, but a scarlet fireball bloomed behind them. I snapped them open again.

The Station was almost empty, but that was to be expected. There were two types of people in Manhattan that night. The strong ones were down there, tearing through bodies and ash. I fell into the other category.

"Well, I have to think about these things," said Samantha. "It's horrible, but people will still have to earn a living." Her right hand clenched and opened, over and over. I don't think she noticed. "You know you and I will be left with most of the work come Thursday. Everyone else will stay home."

My eyes drifted to the window behind her. Lots of trendy bars shelled out thousands for brass fixtures, wood paneling, reprints of vintage Coca–Cola signs… anything to create an old–timey atmosphere. The Station, however, actually was old, and therefore unpopular. The glass of the window was thick and greenish, with tiny bubbles in its corners. Its surface swelled in random spots at the edges. My reflection in it was swollen and distorted. I moved my head. Leaning to the right made me look like a broccoli–headed freak. Bobbing to the left squished me into an Oompa Loompa.

Samantha glanced at the watch on her left hand, her right one still opening and closing. "I have to get going," she said. I took a slow sip of Jack. It burned my throat the same way I burned all over. I looked up to say goodbye.

I saw my first Autumn Person.

She was inside the window, her stick–like reflection floating behind Samantha's. She was tall, slender, and wore flowing robes that seemed to be part of her glistening skin. She placed a long hand on Samantha's shoulder. She stared at me as she caressed Samantha's hair, her eyes amber swirls of fire. Her mouth pleaded the word "no."

"I'll see you Thursday. Don't be late," said Samantha, oblivious to the thing stroking her reflection. She stood, pulling a cracked leather purse over the shoulder of her slate and cream ensemble.

I bolted out of the chair, almost knocking it over. I grabbed her hand, the one that was still having spasms. We stood like that until her fingers stopped their frantic dance, and clutched mine. The thing in the window screamed like my... as if I were the monster instead. I led Samantha outside to her Volkswagen. We drove to her apartment in silence.

The moment her door closed behind us, I pinned her up against it. She clamped her mouth to mine, the manicured fingers of one hand digging into my shoulder while the other fumbled with the button on my jeans. My hands found her neck, her breasts, her waist, and the hem of her skirt. We stood, stroking each other, our kisses becoming more frantic with the intensity of each other's caresses. I yanked her pantyhose down as she wiggled out of her shoes, and wrapped her arms around my neck. I crumpled her grey, professional skirt up around her waist, and pulled her up against me. Finally, after years of dreaming, we made a frantic, violent love against the painted steel.

I woke somewhere around two, cradling Samantha in my arms. I had worked for her for three years now, and I knew maybe a fraction of her life. Every day, I saw the toll it had etched upon her face. But asleep, she almost looked like a child. She almost looked like someone whose mother hadn't run off when she was five, whose fiancé hadn't left when she was twenty, someone who hadn't missed opportunity after opportunity, and was wasting her talents away in a record store. She almost didn't look like a woman who needed a torrent of shots every other night to be able to sleep. Almost.

My arm stung from lack of circulation. I pulled it out as gently as I could from underneath her shoulders. I stroked her auburn hair, trying to ignore the ball of anxiety swelling in my chest. One–night stands were the opposites of the window in The Station; they stretched out sex until it looked like love. But in the morning, reality always waits outside of the funhouse.

What would Pop have said about all this? He sure as hell wouldn't be hiding in someone's bed. If he were still alive, he would be at Ground Zero, tearing bloody concrete aside with his bare hands until he freed the survivors. He wouldn't have stood like an idiot as a black cloud poured down and smothered the streets, as the sky rained ash, fire, and bodies, watching as people jumped out of the windows to escape the inferno, just watching them fall, screaming, some holding hands like frightened children —

I pressed my hands against my eyes, trying to squeeze the memory out. Yeah, if Pop were alive, he'd be down there along with every other jackhammer jockey in the city. As far as my mother went, well, her Catholic sensibilities would be shattered — as if she had any sensibilities left.

Something in my eyes burned and spilled down my cheeks. My tongue hurt. I must have chewed on it. I slipped out of bed, tucking Samantha into her lumpy, faded comforter. For a moment, I could pretend that the funhouse mirror was real, that we were in love, that I could take care of her. It didn't last long. I had to go to the bathroom.

The Autumn Woman waited for me in the darkness, in a spotted mirror surrounded by paint that was cracked and peeling. I flicked on the light. It washed most of her image away, but a ghost remained. I turned it off again, and she returned. She stared into my eyes, and shook her head. She raised a robed hand, and pointed to the door. I opened it.

Above Samantha's dresser was a mirror, and in the dim streetlight I saw a different version of the studio: a clean room, with bright paint instead of peeling wallpaper, and indigo curtains instead of grimy blinds on the windows. The only things that didn't belong in that dream room were its flawed occupants. The Autumn Woman walked over to Samantha's reflection. She leaned in and kissed her, her lips brushing Samantha's cheek.

She raised her head. Her eyes flowed with tears of silver. Then she touched Samantha's belly.

Samantha's face contorted, as if living through some sudden nightmare. She lurched up, clutching her abdomen. She pushed past me, ran into the bathroom, and slammed the door behind her. I asked her if she was ok, but she would not answer.

"What did you do?" I asked the mirror, but the insect–woman and her reflection utopia were gone. Only a dingy studio remained, with Samantha panting and sobbing behind the bathroom door. I asked her again if something was wrong, and if she needed privacy.

"I'm bleeding," she said.

It took me a moment to understand. "Oh," I said. "Look, if you want me to step out, or, um, go to a drug store —"

"No," she gasped. "It's way too much, and it's two weeks early. It hurts so bad —" Her voice choked off. I grabbed my phone out of my pants pocket, and called 911.

They wouldn't tell me anything at the hospital; they just let me sit on a folding chair. Every half hour or so, they answered my questions with more questions. No, I didn't know any of her relatives. Was it that serious? Yes. Could I see her, just for a moment? Were we married? Engaged? Then no.

After six hours, an intern took pity on me. Tumors, he said, tumors in her uterus. They had bled. They weren't malignant, thank God, but Samantha could never have children now. My heart dropped. Even though I never had been big on kids, I knew that she wanted them, in a far—off Someday. I took her keys from her purse before turning it over to the hospital. I took the subway back to her apartment, and let myself in.

I looked around her studio. I'm not one of those guys who carries a condom around in his wallet in the hope that he'll get lucky. (I tried that once and the damn thing exploded, making a gooey mess out of the one and only fifty dollar leather wallet I had ever owned.) We had talked a few times about our previous exploits, circling our wagons around each other. She'd said that she always insisted on being protected. I had said the same thing, but it wasn't true, it was just something you say to sound responsible. But I didn't remember putting anything on that night. I searched her garbage can, the floor, and the sheets. I found nothing, not even a wrapper.

I turned the lights off, and closed the blinds. I walked to the dresser mirror. I stood in front of it for a long time, squinting, trying to force a vision out of the glass. There was nothing there, just a low—rent studio in a bad part of Brooklyn.

"You only did that because I got her pregnant, didn't you?" I asked. But nothing replied.

That night, I returned to the hospital, and they allowed me to see her. She sat propped up in bed, watching the never–ending news coverage. A woman with a face like a walnut snored in the bed next to hers. Samantha looked at me with red, puffy eyes. "My keys," she said, her voice dull.

"Here," I said, handing them over. She made sure not to touch my hand as she took them, and I knew she had joined the ranks of my victims: poor, sweet, innocent girls I had supposedly taken advantage of in their weakest moments. I tried to be angry, but I couldn't. She actually did have a reason to hate me, even if she didn't know it.

I volunteered to take her home but she said no, her sister was coming, and would look after her. She said the National Guard had closed off lower Manhattan, and that I should try to collect unemployment until we could work again. I told her to get better, and to please call me. I tried to kiss her goodbye, but she turned her face so I'd only have her cheek. Sometimes, my stupidity astounds me.

I showered, slept, ate, and tried to bear the loneliness of the next day. I needed to do something more than just hang around my apartment, wafting in the aroma of the sewage pipe backing up in the basement. I couldn't bear to be alone, even if it meant seeking out another funhouse mirror.

I ventured into the city. The MTA was handling the crisis with their usual efficiency: it took me an hour to go ten miles. The stench hit me when I got off of the E train. Even in Midtown, the air reeked of charred people. A pillar of smoke loomed in the southern sky, waiting for the right moment to topple, and smother us all.

The Village Voice defines Eclipse as a cross between MoMA and an acid trip. The feminists of New York classify it under meat market. But as the old man said in *Citizen Kane,* if you just want to make money, there's no trick to it.

Well, maybe a few tricks.

The atmosphere of Eclipse was a deliberate contrast to that of The Station and its trendy imitators. Black lights flashed to the beat of music with the bass cranked so high, I couldn't tell if it was Chopin or Cradle of Filth. Escher and Dali prints hung on the walls at skewed angles. Every few feet a bizarre sculpture, probably a third place winner in a high school art show, adorned the magenta–tiled floor.

I honed in on a girl sitting alone in a booth. She was voluptuous, her round face framed with a mop of blond hair that looked like she had cut it herself. Dark circles under her eyes peeked out from gaps in her foundation. An oversized t–shirt bearing John Lennon's face hung off one naked shoulder. It glowed violet under the black lights. She took a long drag from a menthol cigarette, staring off into space.

I strode over, armed with a gentle smile and eye contact. She looked up at me, and I could see the red inflammation around her button nose. She almost returned my smile as I sat on the hard plastic seat across from her. She pulled out a new cigarette and my hand was there, Zippo open and ignited. The old tricks may be old, but they work.

I asked her if she was a Dali fan, because the print above our booth was *The Temptation of St. Anthony*. "Dolly who?" she wanted to know, brushing her hand against mine. I was about to subtly point out the use of erotic imagery in surrealist art, when I saw my second Autumn Person.

His face was long and jagged, like that of a mantis. His visage held no beauty, just hateful, amber eyes that said they would kill me if I made him do *that* to this woman. He loomed behind her in the Plexiglas wall of the booth. Slowly, he spread out wings that were thin, veined, and translucent. I thought for a moment that they must be hard and crunchy. I stood, gnawing away at my tongue. I ran, leaving my trusty Zippo behind. The moment I was through the door, I threw up on the sidewalk.

I staggered to Port Authority, and cleaned myself up in the urine–scented bathroom. I took a long, hard look in the filthy mirror. *What do I have to do,* I wondered, *chop my balls off?*

I went back home. I turned the radio to 1010 WINS, and turned the volume down until the newscasters' voices were incoherent mumbles. I lay in bed with the lights on, and the pillowcase over my eyes. Another trick. It almost seemed like someone was there in the room, talking to me. With enough alcohol in my veins, I would have believed it.

I dreamt of The City.

Its air was clean and sweet. Towers of crystal arched around and through one another. Each structure was a sculpture, each design flowing with elegance and grace. Millions strode along its streets. They were healthy and strong, their eyes clear and shining with purpose.

They were happy.

Without warning, the city began to run backwards, like a film in reverse. The people became either bloated or scrawny, their skin sallow, their faces twisted with pain. The crystal exteriors of the towers splintered away as if just a facade, revealing concrete skyscrapers beneath. Graffiti demanding death, a screw, or both, scribbled itself across their walls. Automobiles choked the streets, their horns and alarms blaring as they drove backwards.

With a jerk, the film rolled forward again.

The city burst into white flame. Its people splintered like dry kindling. A mushroom cloud bloomed in the center of the metropolis, rising into the burning sky.

The film froze, pausing the cloud in mid–incineration. Then the film ran backwards again, and the mushroom deflated.

A swarm of roaches spewed from the reversing billows. They swept me in their tide as the charred meat around me reformed into human beings, as the buildings swept back into existence. Time flowed back a few more decades.

Then it happened again.

And again.

Each time the mushrooms shrank, the insects grew in number.

Time rolled backwards, and the roaches marched along with it. I watched the faces around me, and smelled the changes in the air. I knew the Time was coming.

The world played forward again.

I scanned the sky for the first of two passenger jets. It wasn't long before it appeared, flying low, much too low, on the horizon.

The Towers fell.

They rose again, sucked back from blood, rubble, and fire.

The army of insects carried me through the East River as the years peeled away. We marched back onto dry land, and into Queens.

They led me to a tiny office, a diorama inside of a shoebox. A calendar, drawn on the wall in crayon, marked the year as 1968. A G.I. Joe action figure, wearing a hard hat and holding a tiny jackhammer in his Kung Fu Grip, sat behind a desk.

A headless Barbie doll entered the office, résumé in hand. The stream of roaches marched backwards into her neck, and down her body. She became bloated with them, her body expanding, but never bursting. I could see the insects pushing out against it, making her plastic skin thinner every second, crawling over one another, seething just below her malleable flesh, and I screamed and screamed.

I let the same nightmare torture me for three nights. Then I went to see her.

"Who are you?" asked the woman behind the desk. I told her my name, and whom I was there to visit. I expected some sort of indignation, at least a narrowing of the eyes. Pop was the only one who ever visited her, and he had been dead for a year. But the nurse just shrugged, and pointed me towards the day room.

She was strapped to a chair, staring with dead eyes at the television set, along with ten other zombies. I wondered if that was the cruelest punishment of all, having to stare at the idiot box day in and day out. Her hair was silky, like a baby's. Her mouth had a tiny grin frozen on it. It gave her pitted cheeks dimples, as if she were a middle–aged Cabbage Patch doll.

"Hi, Mom," I said. The demented gnome in the chair next to her chirped, "Help me, help me," over and over, her jaw slack, her eyes blank. No one paid any attention to her. I wished she would shut the fuck up.

"Well, Mom, I'll be here with you soon," I said. I pulled an empty chair over, and sat down. I glanced at the television, chewing my tongue absentmindedly. "I guess I'd better catch up on the story, huh?"

My mother just sat there, staring ahead. The smile became a sharp V, and a thin line of yellow dribble flowed down her chin. Pop hadn't known about the time bomb lurking inside her head when he married her. Whenever I think of my childhood, I always picture my mother crying, and trying to hide it. I saw her smack her face once or twice when she thought no one was looking. But a kid doesn't know what those things mean.

Somewhere along the line, she became afraid of mirrors.

One day when I was seven, I came home from school, and saw her crouching under the table in the dining room. She was eating roaches. They were trying to get out, crawling around her mouth as her teeth crunched on their hard shells. She screamed when I tried to get her to stop. She screamed that she was eating them so they wouldn't hurt me. Pop had to commit her, and it wasn't long before she ran away to somewhere safe inside of her own skull. Hereditary, the doctors said. They had checked state records.

My grandfather had been committed when he was forty–two. He died strapped to a bed, just like Mom was strapped to a chair, electrocuted when someone spilled his coffee while administering shock treatments. Grandma ran off to California, leaving baby Mom in the care of her sister and her husband. No one ever heard from her again.

A tall candy striper came over with a plate of strained peas and pureed chicken chunks, and asked if I wanted to feed Mom. "No," I said. "Why should I?"

The girl's jaw dropped open, and shut with a snap. "Well, then," she said, sitting down. She ignored me as she cared for my mother; in goes the spoon, out comes the spoon, here's a napkin to wipe away the dribble. The volunteer's long, raven–colored hair swirled about her shoulders every time she moved. Her skin was the color of cream. I watched the way she brushed my mother's corn silk wisps out of her face, making little "tsk" noises. My throat felt like something was squeezing it. I was about to apologize, when I saw it.

Something glared at me from over her shoulder, something jagged and spindly, with cockroach–like wings. It didn't need a mirror, it was *here*.

I leaped out of my chair, knocking the tray of mush all over my mother. I could make out the outline of the Autumn Man's face, a face that had wide–set eyes just like the candy striper's, but a square chin like mine.

I ran to the street. They were everywhere now, looking over the shoulders of the women gabbing on the street corner, guarding the lady smoking a cigarette as she crossed the intersection, looming behind the girl checking her cell phone messages. The Autumn People all glared at me, some with eyes that belonged to their mothers, some with eyes that were mine. All the nothings, the haven't–beens, the descendants of mine that God, Krishna, or whoever had deemed the cosmos would be better off without. I ran down the stairs to the subway, and leaped over the turnstile. Somebody shouted at me, but I kept running. An express train thundered by on the uptown track, and I had to jump to catch it in time.

I caught it.

I wander through the dust, always moving forward. I've been here for a second, a year, or maybe a century. Time doesn't matter. Some souls appear, and blink, they're gone. Others… well, I once saw two men in goatskins, circling each other, and screaming for Baal. The fog is dry and omnipresent, like a hungry, burning sponge. It's set my eyes aflame, baked my skin to a hard, glistening armor, and twisted my limbs into emaciated twigs.

Each of us has his or her own way out. Once you find it, once you've seen what's beyond, it's always right behind you. You always have to walk forward. You can't turn around. Otherwise, you're there.

None of the other wanderers will speak to me. "What happens?" I ask every soul I meet. "What happens when I leave?" Of course, I know. I just want someone to tell me that it's not true.

My exit leads to an office with walls of fake wood paneling, circa 1968. A man sits behind a desk, holding some paperwork in his large, calloused hands. He is a Korean War veteran with two bronze stars. Although he is only forty, his hair is gray at the temples. He has just started his own construction company.

He is frozen in time. A job applicant has just walked in through the door, a beautiful eighteen–year–old secretary with Catholic sensibilities, and a time bomb in her skull. I know that he's fallen in love with her. I know that she's checking her reflection in the window over his shoulder. I know she can't see me.

But the moment I walk backwards through that cloud, she will.

ABOUT THE AUTHOR

Tony LaRocca is a carbon–based life form, animator, occasional actor, U.S. Army veteran, blogger, karaoke crooner, electrician, and chronic doodler from Basking Ridge, New Jersey. He currently resides with his family in Queens, New York. Please visit him at www.EgotisticalProductions.com. He has lasagna.

OTHER WORKS

Debris of Shadows Book I: The Lies of the Sage

"This story is a breakneck ride through a dark landscape illuminated by flashes of lightning that slowly reveal a complex and surprising world. I can usually see where a story is going, but not this time."

"I was instantly imported into the old/new world and able to picture it perfectly with the detailed descriptions. This author can really paint a picture with words bringing you right into the story."

"While the environment in this story seems so unfathomable, LaRocca's descriptive narrative takes you there without question, and with great emotion, drama, and suspense."

In the late twenty–first century, North America is a divided continent. NorMec is a nation of prosperity, while the West is a wasteland, ravaged by metallic insects that devour everything in their path.

Alyanna Galbraith is one of NorMec's most sought–after *zhivoi*–painters: artists who create living works of artificial intelligence. But when the enigmatic Cylebs take notice, she finds herself and her son trapped within a cybernetic world of imagination — one from which they may never escape.

Debris of Shadows Book II: The Forgotten Cathedral

"I very much enjoyed this book. Twisted, yes. Dark, yes. Leaving you wanting more — YES!… The descriptions of the scenes and action were spot on and I can imagine the worlds he created."

"LaRocca has done it again. In Debris of Shadows Book II: The Forgotten Cathedral, I was immersed in a fictitious world so deeply and vividly, that when I stopped reading, I needed a moment to reacquaint myself to the real world"

"Tony is a wonderful writer with the ability to make his characters come alive. You'll find yourself caring for them and compelled to keep reading about this dark and scary future world where cybernetic bugs are waging war against humans. The story is compelling with many twists and turns involving virtual reality, humans, bugs and artificial life forms."

In a war–ravaged future, Western America is a wasteland swarming with ravenous, cybernetic insects. Its few human survivors reside within computer–generated realities, unaware of their fate.

Matthew Galbraith is an artificial intelligence from NorMec. Sent by the Cylebs in the East, he must search an ever–changing virtual world for a way to save his family and their home. But to learn the secrets of the past, he must first survive a living nightmare where even his soul can be rewritten.

SHORT STORIES

"Just One of Those Human Things"

"Some great dark science fiction with an awesome sense of humor."

"Brilliant as always."

"An excellent story filled with sci–fi, humor, and satire. Read this. You'll thank me."

Sir Aloysius, last of the humans, has been roaming the Moon for 235 years. But when his pet cyborg goes missing, he finds that humanity lies in the tentacles of the beholder.

"Fishers of Men"

"Written in a noir style, this is one fun read. The story involves a priest, alternate universes, bible verses, and a whole lot of blood."

"This is such a fun read. One of my favorite short stories by Tony LaRocca."

"This story is pure delight. It's fun and entertaining with everything a good science fiction story should have — murder, betrayal, and giant fish hooks."

Father Parrino never imagined that a simple deviation in scripture could fracture the walls of reality. But when members of his flock are ripped from the streets and tossed into unhallowed waters, he learns that sometimes, a shepherd must take the divine law into his own hands.